A LIFE *of* DREAMS

A LIFE *of* DREAMS

A NOVEL

DOUG DUNNEVANT

atmosphere press

◇ **1** ◇

Marcus Aurelius

The tidy brick rancher built in 1952 at 16 Jennings Lane was on its third roof by the time Percy had inherited it from his parents, Gilbert and Frances Hope. His troubling dreams had begun as soon as he moved back into the place. His bedroom was the old junk room in the back left hand corner of the house. He could never feel right about using the master bedroom. Instead, he had converted it into a library. The junk room was smaller, barely large enough for his bed, nightstand and dresser, but plenty big enough for his outsized dreams. His old bedroom was part of history now. No way could he live there again. The junk room would have to do.

On the day that his parents passed, he was 37 years old and in desperate need of a break. Although he had genuine affection for them and was distraught at their deaths, his resulting inheritance as their only child had saved his life. He had the house free and clear, and was now in possession of a fairly sizable portfolio, one serviceable late model automobile and a practically brand new pickup truck. It had surprised him that his father had managed to save so much money on a shipping manager's salary. The happy discovery only served

3

to magnify his own financial failures, so his newfound wealth was bittersweet.

Still, at night in his bed he would lay in the darkness and wonder why they never moved out of such a tiny house with all that money in the bank. Why had they not traveled? Why had they chosen to buy a Honda Accord and a Dodge Ram truck? Why had they not bought any new furniture over the last 20 years of their lives? No wonder they had so much money, he thought, they never bought anything. He remembered the trauma that had gripped them when they finally broke down and bought a dryer three years ago. Frances, at 74, was finding it increasingly difficult to lug the laundry out back to the clothesline. After weeks of agonizing indecision, Gilbert showed up one night after work with a Kenmore dryer strapped into the bed of his rusted-out Datsun pickup truck, the one on its second rebuilt engine and about to trip 300,000 miles on the odometer. Percy had come over to help set it up and explain how it worked. After initial skepticism, Fannie eventually fell in love with her new "miracle" machine. Such had been the lives of his parents, hoarding away every penny, doing without modern conveniences out of fear that a coming financial storm would wipe them out. Now their only son was plagued by dreams.

There was Gilbert standing at the dark end of a long hallway in a tuxedo, the thin moist line of a tear tracing from the corner of his right eye down to the edge of his mouth. It was a still image of the only time he had ever seen his father cry, the moment he and Beth had turned around to face the crowd on their wedding day after being pronounced husband and wife. It had so astonished him that the money shot of the wedding photographs was ruined for posterity by his shaken expression. Friends, many years after the fact, would remember the picture as an omen. But now, Gilbert just stood in the hall, frozen in time, unapproachable and silent as a stone.

On other nights it would be Beth standing provocatively at

the door to the junk room wearing one of his dress shirts, tugging on her bottom lip. She never spoke and never approached the bed, just stood there reminding him of the first passionate months and how something like fevered sexual madness had consumed them both. It was not altogether nightmarish. But it was troubling, since he had held her in such contempt since the divorce; it was difficult to imagine her as something desirable. On this night, she spoke.

"I've missed you, Percy," she whispered, leaning her head against the door frame. "In so many ways you were a terrible husband, such a miserable provider, so lacking in ambition... but still, I've missed you. Absence has made my heart grow fonder."

Then she vanished, and the blue pinstriped oxford floated slowly to the floor.

Gilbert knew. His quiet, emotionless father had known what his son was getting into. That's why he shed the one tear of his entire existence the very minute it was all official, in front of friends and in the presence of God. He knew what was coming, but hadn't bothered to breathe a word of this foreboding intuition to his son when it might have done some good. It wasn't his place to butt in, he would explain later, after Percy had lost everything.

Percy had been surprised when Beth showed up at the funeral home. An electric charge of dread had silenced the room when she walked in, stopping family and friends in mid-sentence of their hushed conversations. Percy had glanced up in the silence and seen her signing the guest register. He was instantly overcome with grief and the tears flowed like a river to the great dismay of the gathered mourners. Beth dropped the pen and ran to his side. She held him as he wept and said not a word.

A couple of weeks after the funeral and after Percy had moved into the house on 16 Jennings Lane, she dropped by unannounced with a pound cake. Percy had let her in, and they stood awkwardly in the living room in the exact spot where they had stood the night that he had brought her to meet the parents 12 years earlier. On that night she had worn a yellow sun dress and was a vision, a feast for the eyes. Even Gilbert had been taken aback by the sight of her. Now, she wore a pair of jeans and a sleeveless sky blue blouse, looking older and more serious. Percy thanked her for the cake and watched her drive away in the Mercedes C-Class sedan she had taken from him in the divorce. Two nights later, the dreams had begun.

Lately he had taken up reading the classics as they offered a passage to the past, which, for Percy, was always a better place than the present. After dinner and after darkness fell, he would turn on the fluorescent desk lamp in his parents' old bedroom, and slip into the guilty comfort of his brand new Herman Miller Aeron chair. It was the first thing he had bought with his inheritance. Gilbert would have died a second death if he knew how much money he had spent. But, the lines were elegant, and he could sit for hours without as much as a shift of weight from one side of his ass to the other. This sort of ergonomic perfection was essential now that he spent most of his time rummaging through the wisdom of the ancients. Tonight it was the Meditations of Marcus Aurelius. Ten minutes in, Beth appeared at the door.

"What are you reading?" she asked without any hint of genuine curiosity. The hall light shone directly behind her head and seemed to set her red hair on fire. Percy looked up, coolly annoyed, and asked, "Why do you keep doing this? How did you get in here?"

"I have the key to your heart, remember? What are you reading?"

"Nothing that would interest you."

"Don't be so sure, darling. I've made a lot of changes since the divorce. I've actually started reading a lot myself." She walked over and lifted the book from his hands. "Meditations of Marcus Aurelius? Really, Percy?"

"I admit, it's not exactly Fifty Shades of Grey. I told you that you wouldn't be interested."

"Don't knock Shades, Percy. I would wager that EL James has sold more books than this Aurelius egghead ever thought about selling. Oh, I'm sorry. Forgive me for using the word 'wager' around you. That was an accidental slip of the tongue. I apologize."

Nothing Beth had ever done with her tongue was accidental. It never took her very long in any of their conversations to get around to his gambling. She had a gift, a sinister ability to turn the knife without ever drawing blood.

"Would you please leave?"

"I'll only leave when you truly want me to."

"Suit yourself."

Beth turned her back and walked over to the loveseat that Percy had put in the spot where his dad's old chest of drawers had sat for 40 years. She sat down gracefully and folded her legs beneath her. "Comfy."

Percy worked hard to block her out, using all his powers of concentration on the noble pagan emperor. Suddenly the words jumped off the page and began flying around the room. His face lit up with discovery and his eyes brightened. "You want to know why I read Aurelius? I'll tell you why... *I have often wondered how it is that every man loves himself more than all the rest of men and yet sets less value on his own opinions of himself than on the opinions of others.*'"

"If Marcus Aurelius was so freaking moral, how come he persecuted the early Christians with such brutality?"

"Wait... what?"

"That's right, Percy. You weren't the only one who took ancient history in college, you arrogant prick!"

Percy stared at Beth a little longer than was comfortable, then said, "Well, like many great thinkers, Aurelius struggled with consistency."

"Do you ever think about us? Sometimes I think we gave

up too easily. Ever think about giving it another shot?"

"You're insane! A minute ago I was an arrogant prick, and now you want to get back together?"

"... Like many great thinkers, I struggle with consistency."

Percy couldn't help but smile. This was vintage Beth. No one could flip the switch from she-devil to Aphrodite quicker than his ex-wife.

"Since you started it, wasn't it also Marcus Aurelius who said... '*accept the things to which fate binds you, and love the people with whom fate brings you together, but do so with all your heart.*' That's us Percy. You and I are bound together by fate, but we never loved each other with all of our hearts."

"I truly want you to leave now."

"Ok."

Her image melted into the atmosphere, and the only thing that remained was the scent of her perfume.

What bothered Percy the most about the dreams was the timing. The events leading up to the end of things, his crippling gambling losses, her infidelity, and the bitterness of the divorce proceedings themselves had left him nearly fatally wounded. He had descended into an overwhelmingly deep and forsaken hole. Gilbert and Frances had stood vigil as best they could; paying for one therapist after another until, at long last, the fog lifted, and Percy was able to carve out something close to a life for himself. Once he had recovered enough to start that life, he was 35 years old and out of money. Part of the fallout from his breakdown had been the loss of his associate professorship at UVA teaching English Literature. He had landed at a community college. It was dreadful and didn't pay very much, but now, finally, money wasn't an issue.

Since the inheritance, he had settled in nicely to his life and hadn't placed a bet in 26 months and 14 days. So, why was Beth back? How had he let her back inside his head? The truth was, he thought about her all day, not just when she appeared in his dreams. The fact that she would ask him that question in a dream seemed important somehow. He didn't like this new Beth, the one who had begun to talk.

◆ **2** ◆

The Gift

They had met at the Borgata Hotel and Casino in Atlantic City, not a story they looked forward to telling their future children. Beth was there as part of a bachelorette weekend, Percy was there to gamble. He saw her standing behind a fairly drunk girl wearing a tiara at the roulette table. She was so beautiful he couldn't bring himself to look away. Luckily she was oblivious, so Percy spent 30 minutes watching her every move discreetly from behind one of the faux Corinthian columns that held up the faux crystal and diamond studded ceiling. Suddenly, in the midst of some boisterous joke that had propelled the entire bridal party into uproarious laughter, Beth looked up from the roulette wheel directly into his eyes. Instead of glancing quickly away, she held her gaze. Percy later remembered feeling as if he had been frozen in time, unable or unwilling to look away. Even in the gaudy, unnatural light of a casino, he could see that her eyes were green, green eyes and red hair, the ancient sign of the witch.

Witch or not, she was the first woman who had ever had the power to distract him from the games for more than two seconds. She walked around the table, through the crowds, and stopped an uncomfortably creepy 12 inches from his face.

"My name is Beth. You've been staring at me for the past half hour, so I thought the least I could do was tell you my name. Like what you see?"

Percy Hope hadn't been this physically close to a woman this beautiful in all of his 24 years, and words would not come. He just latched on to those mysterious eyes and managed a smile. She smiled back and he noticed the perfect teeth, a light dusting of freckles, and the sweet smell of vodka and perfume.

"Well, don't I even get a name?"

Percy regained his composure long enough to take half a step back and form the word "Percy" without further embarrassment.

Beth took a half step forward while blurting out, "Seriously?! Percy? Who names their kid Percy? So, what? Are you rich? Only rich kids get named Percy!"

If he had his wits about him, he would have been offended, but Percy was so gratified to be the focus of this goddess's attention that she could have questioned his sexual orientation, and he wouldn't have batted an eye. Then she did.

"The kinds of people who name their son Percy usually have names like Gilbert and Frances." Percy was pleased with himself for saying something that wasn't entirely stupid.

"You're not gay are you?"

"Gay? No! Why... what, why would you think that?"

"Because I'm the most gorgeous thing you've ever been this close to in your life, and you haven't tried to kiss me yet."

It would always be this way with Beth. She always knew his thoughts, could read his mind as if it wasn't even his, like it was opened up to her and her alone. From the moment they had met in the surreal atmosphere of an Atlantic City casino, Percy Hope would never again have a private thought.

She sat with him the next night at the blackjack table for 3 hours and watched him win $14,800. They celebrated by sleeping together. Thus began a whirlwind eight-month romance that had culminated in a simple Baptist wedding with a conspicuously lavish reception at the Jefferson Hotel. More than one guest had wondered quietly where on earth Percy Hope had found a woman with such extravagant tastes, not to mention how in heaven's name he could afford such a soiree since Beth had been given away by a "cousin" no older than Percy and about which very little was known or offered, with no parents anywhere in sight. It had been quite the scandal.

What no one knew was that Percy had gotten his money from an uncanny predilection for winning games of chance. It had started in college when he had found himself being accused of cheating by his dorm mates for winning all the football pools. Then he was blacklisted by a Philadelphia bookie. The last straw had been Percy winning an over/under bet when an extra point attempt was blocked with 40 seconds to play at the end of an Eagles-Cowboys game. Whether it was clairvoyance or just dumb, blind luck, his virtually uninterrupted four-year winning streak had paid for his last two years of college, all of grad school, and the first mind-numbing year of his marriage. Beth loved everything about their life together. She seemed to be placed into this world to live the high life.

By the time of their first anniversary, things had begun to change. It was one thing to win enough money to pay tuition bills and put yourself through school, another thing entirely to win money that financed mere epicurean delight. Percy was beginning to tire of the sound of jackpot bells, the click and bing of tokens spilling into metal trays. The recycled oxygen and fluorescent lighting were wearing on him. The old ladies' slumped shoulders at the slots weighed upon his heart somehow. Most surprising of all, Percy had begun to feel an embarrassment of riches. His luck had now taken on the whiff of scandal. It's not like the house could catch him cheating, because he wasn't cheating. Besides, his luck extended to every game he played. He was forced to intentionally lose at blackjack and poker to make it look good. After four years of winning, gambling now seemed more like stealing, and since the possibility of ruin didn't seem in play, the rush of it all had vanished. Percy had tired of his life, this perpetual party. He wanted to go back to school and get his doctorate, he wanted to write, read, and settle into the scholarly life he had always wanted. He wanted to think about starting a family. None of this could be done from a high roller suite at Caesars Palace. As was the case with everything else, Beth already knew.

On a flight back from Vegas, Beth sat at the window seat twirling the ice in her Diet Coke around with her index finger, one of several irritating personal idiosyncrasies Percy had discovered in their first year together. She had been quiet for most of the trip, then blurted out, "Why do you stop?"

"Stop what?"

"Stop playing? You could win all the money in the world. You have a gift. Why stop?"

"How much did we win this time?" Percy asked, trying to change the subject.

"After expenses, about $25,000." Beth always knew to the penny.

"Guess I feel a little guilty. Besides, there's got to be more to life than this." Percy shocked himself by this rare admission of truth.

Beth turned fully towards him with genuine affection, reached out and caressed his face. "Oh, Percy..." It was always difficult to read Beth Hope. He felt relatively sure that she loved him on some level, but he never could be sure how deeply committed she was to him. There had always been a lost quality to her, like she was never quite fully in the moment. About the time he thought she was on the edge of a serious thought, some inane triviality would come flying out of her mouth. Other times, when her shallow foolishness was becoming too much to bear, she would tear up and quote a line of French poetry. Percy never could decide whether it was an act or just evidence of amazing mental versatility.

"Of course there's more to life than this, darling." Her eyes were moist with tears. "There's... Monte Carlo."

The tipping point had come several weeks later during dinner with his parents. Gilbert and Frances tried very hard to like Beth. They accepted her into the family without reservation, but it was an acceptance of fact rather than of the heart. Sometimes when Beth was going on and on about a topic that was borderline inappropriate, Gilbert's mouth would hang open ever so slightly and he would take on the appearance of an anthropologist who had stumbled upon Sasquatch talking on a cell phone. Although Gilbert and Frances knew that their son gambled, Percy had kept the detail of his supernatural luck a secret. After Frances had served a dessert of homemade cherry pastry with vanilla ice cream, Gilbert broached the subject.

"Percy, your mother and I had hoped that once you and Beth got settled in after the wedding, you would stop spending so much time going to the casinos, but if anything, it seems that you have been going even more. I must say that we have been disappointed."

Beth cut a sideways glance at Percy who made no immediate reply. Finally, after a sip of coffee, Percy managed a defense, "Come on, Pop. We're newlyweds. We enjoy spending time with each other. You know, it's very cheap to fly to Vegas and the hotels are practically free after all the discounts."

"Besides, Gilbert." Beth interrupted with a devious smile. "Your son is quite an accomplished gambler. Every weekend we bring home close to 25 grand."

Frances' fork slipped out of her hand and bounced off the edge of her dessert plate. Gilbert abruptly sat up straight in his chair looking horrified. "Is this true, Percy? $25,000??"

For the first time in his marriage, Percy was furious with his wife. He quickly throttled back the indignation, gathered himself and lied, "Now wait a minute Pop. Sure, every now and then I have a good run, but I don't win that kind of money all the time."

"That's right," Beth jumped in. "Sometimes we win more! What's the problem Gilbert? I would have thought you would have been thrilled to learn that Percy was good at something besides marrying a hot wife."

"Percy, gambling money is cursed!" Gilbert stood up from the table. "It's an ill-gotten gain, son. Nothing good can come from it."

"Actually, a lot of good things have come from it – Percy's education for one thing." Beth had changed the tone of her voice from rowdy to reasonable in an instant. "Now, I understand that your feelings against gambling are strong, but Percy isn't breaking any laws. We pay our taxes. He just happens to be one hell of a card player. He has a gift, and that gift is making us both very happy. Now Gilbert, sit down and let's finish this cherry dessert, which, by the way Frances, is to die for."

On the drive home, Percy was silent. While Beth went on and on about the events of the evening, Percy made the quiet decision to never place another bet.

◇ 3 ◇

Sam

It had been a beautiful night, one of those mid April spring evenings before the pollen had come, before the winds had cast a dewy yellow film over the earth. Percy had found some khaki shorts knotted up in his chest of drawers along with a UVA tee shirt. He dug out the flip flops from the back of his closet, and within minutes had a steak cooking on the grill on the back deck. He poured himself a beer and listened to the sizzle of the meat on the low gas flame. There was a bird, loud and rhythmic, singing from the top of one of the huge pines in the back yard.

He was alone, and trying to come to grips with being alone. He had taken the time to reconnect with some friends from the church he had been a member of for most of his life. It was more accurate to say that it was his parents' church, but it was also his, if in a less consuming way. He had stopped going when he was married to accommodate Beth, and honestly hadn't missed it much, although it had cost him some friendships, friendships that he had started to rebuild by going every other Sunday or so and playing on the softball team. It was strangely uncomfortable at first, but after a while it actually felt nice to be a part of something again, the soft-ball team more so than the church. Pastor Riggs looked 100 years old. He had stood in that same pulpit practically every Sunday for 40 years, and as Percy sat and listened to his first sermon in over a decade, it occurred to him how difficult it must be to come up with something interesting to say after 1800 sermons. For Pastor Riggs it had turned out to be impossible. It was as if Percy had never left, like Riggs just started up where he had left off when Percy had walked away, with some boring story about the children of Israel being disobedient about some such thing and God sending down thunderous judgment upon them. But Riggs was a good man, a kind and loving man, and in the end, that's what the members of Fairview Baptist wanted. They wanted a man who would care for them, who would marry them, bury them, and visit them when they were sick, a man without ambitions. When Percy lay in the hospital after trying to kill himself, Riggs had been there... for his parents. The first words he had spoken to Percy after he had regained consciousness had been to say how he had missed seeing him in church on Sundays. It was what the world was about for Albert Riggs; it was about who was there and who wasn't there, and it was his job to keep score.

The steak was delicious, tasted like the outdoors. After dinner it began to get dark, and Percy sat on the sliding swing looking out over the expansive yard. The clothesline was still strung tightly between two rusted metal T-shaped poles that Gilbert had pounded into the ground with a ten-pound hammer a hundred years ago. There were the mammoth pine trees, at least four feet in diameter, that rimmed the property line in the back, the wild, out of control forsythia bushes blazing in bright yellow that separated Gilbert's yard from the neighbors. Soon the crickets would start to sing, and if Percy closed his eyes it would be like he was 17 again.

He saw him limp out from the forsythias, favoring his left front paw. He didn't recognize the dog from the neighborhood. He looked thin and rough; the way dogs do when they spend all of their time outdoors roaming around. The dog held his head high, the smell of meat in the air, then saw Percy on the deck. He cocked his head to one side as if to get a better look, then began trotting painfully towards the deck. Percy smiled and walked down the steps to get a closer look himself. He looked like some sort of mix, probably some lab in him. His coat was blond, short haired and filthy. No leash, something wrong with one of his ears, like he might have lost part of it in a fight. But despite his pitiful condition, the dog was not afraid or shy; he limped straight up to Percy with bright eyes and what looked like a delirious smile, and laid down right at his feet.

"Well, hello." Percy knelt down and looked more closely to make sure the dog didn't have mange. "What's your name, boy?" The dog sat up and extended his wounded left paw to Percy. "Paw giving you trouble, boy? Got something stuck in there? Let's take a look." A dime sized burr had lodged itself into his paw pad. When Percy tried to remove it, he pricked his own thumb and blood bubbled up quickly. "Damn! No wonder you're limping, boy." Percy ran into the house, found some pliers and a couple of dish rags that he soaked under some warm water from the faucet. When he returned to the deck, the dog had jumped up somehow onto the sliding swing and had his left paw extended out, waiting patiently. One firm tug with the pliers removed the burr, and the dog let out a small yelp, but then jumped down from the swing and walked over towards the grill, nose high and sniffing.

"You look like you could use a meal, boy, but let's clean you up first."

Percy spent the rest of the night reclaiming the dog from neglect. There were scratches all over his legs, his coat was infested with ticks. Percy went to the tool shed and found a metal wash tub, filled it with warm water from the kitchen and gave the dog a bath with his Old Spice body wash. The dog didn't fight the attention and seemed to be overjoyed with the suds. At some point during the bath Percy found himself calling the dog "Sam." It seemed right, seemed to fit the irrepressible spirit of this abused animal. After spraying him off and toweling him down, Percy noticed how thin he was, his ribs tracing curved arches along his sides. "You hungry, Sam?"

Sam raced up on the deck and stood looking through the screen door, tail wagging, as Percy scrounged through the refrigerator looking for something that would serve as dog food. Percy looked back over his shoulder at the dog's grateful face, then reached for the remaining New York Strip. He placed it on the cutting board and sliced it carefully into small squares, then placed them on a plate and sprinkled some grated cheddar cheese on top. He ran some cold water into a large cereal bowl and returned to the deck.

"Sam, I'm not sure if this is the best thing to be feeding a starving dog, but it's either this or frozen pizza."

Percy placed the food and water on the ground in front of Sam, then sat down on the swing expecting a vociferous display of bad eating manners, but Sam looked down at the food, backed up a step and looked back at Percy as if in disbelief. The dog had just been presented with a meal fit for a King, and he had hesitated, taking the time to stare at Percy with eyes wet with what looked like gratitude. "Go ahead and eat, Sam. It's for you boy."

Sam then lunged at the plate and devoured every morsel, licked all the bloody juice clean, and drank the bowl dry. He then gave his new clean body a mighty shake, walked over to the swing and laid down, resting his head on Percy's feet. Percy reached down and scratched the top of his head. "You're a good boy, aren't you Sam?"

Percy would have to ask around the neighborhood tomorrow, see if anyone knew the dog's owner. But for tonight, he would sit on the deck and let this dog warm his toes against the cool breeze. They sat together for the better part of an hour, until it began to get chilly. Percy went inside and found an old blanket in the top of the linen closet, folded it into a three-foot square, then placed it beside the screen door under the green and white striped awning. "You can sleep here tonight, Sam. That way, if it rains, you'll stay dry. Tomorrow, maybe we'll see about getting you a collar and some real dog food, ok buddy?" Percy had already decided that Sam was his now. If he had a previous owner, he couldn't be much of one to allow the dog to reach such a state. All night Percy lay in bed thinking of things to do for Sam. He would build him a doghouse, or maybe even let him sleep inside. He would have to find a vet and get him checked out, of course. It had been years since Percy had had a dog, since high school. He would have to read up on the best dog foods and buy him some toys to play with. Maybe he would have to build a fence to keep him from running off; roaming around free might prove a hard habit to break. He had finally fallen asleep some time after midnight.

The next morning, his eyes opened and for a few minutes he lay awake feeling a strange expectation, an excited brightness, a surprising gratefulness for the day. It was Saturday, or maybe Sunday, whatever, he was going to spend it taking care of his dog, getting to know this amazing gift that had limped into his back yard with the power to infuse his life with an almost electric sense of purpose. Percy bounded out of bed, skipped past the coffee maker to the screen door of the deck and threw it open. Sam was gone.

Percy threw on a jacket and began walking up and down Jennings Lane, calling out a name that was a mere 12 hours old. He didn't expect to find the dog but felt that an effort should be made. In truth, Percy's heart was sick, and he felt overwhelmed by loss. He had only known the dog for a few hours but had been transformed by the responsibility of its care and protection. He had lain awake imagining the possibilities of what adopting a dog might mean for his life, what changes it might work in his character. But, just as he had limped into his life with no warning, now he had returned to his old life, tick-less and smelling of Old Spice. Maybe he would roam around all day out of habit, then return at night for another steak. Or maybe his old abusive owner had found him and thrown him back into a wire cage in a filthy backyard piled high with rusted junk. Either way, it would do no good to worry about it. And yet Percy found himself walking for over an hour, driving slowly in every direction down every adjoining street, looking for any sign of Sam until well after noon. He would finally give up and head home only to find Sam standing on his front porch, ears perked and tail wagging. It was a rush of joy and happiness Percy hadn't experienced since he was eight years old on Christmas morning.

❖ 4 ❖

Harry's

Like almost everything else in his life, the decision to get a dog had been made for him by Sam's fortuitous appearance in his backyard. Percy had been going back and forth on the dog decision for weeks. He knew it would be a time commitment, but he had plenty of that. Even though his new home was small, at night it seemed cavernous and much too quiet. Truth be told, he was lonely. He had no family left, and since the divorce, he had failed to reconnect with many of his old friends. Maybe a dog would help. But after lots of research, he got bogged down in the details, couldn't decide on a breed, and soon the momentum died. But ever since Sam materialized in Percy's back yard he had made himself at home and became the one living thing with which Percy had the majority of his conversations. Although still lonely, Percy now had someone who, while lacking in the conversation department, seemed to have supernatural powers of understanding. Percy would sit out on the deck at night, unloading every frustration and anxiety while Sam lay at his feet in rapt attention, eyebrows raising with each inflection change in Percy's voice. He was just a dog, and a stray at that, but Sam had become the one reliably good thing in his life.

Still, Percy's days had fallen into monotonous rhythm, teaching classes in the afternoons on Tuesdays and Thursdays and in the mornings the other days, with weekends off. He ate his dinners out most nights at his favorite restaurants. He took in an occasional movie, sometimes attended a baseball game, but most nights, by seven o'clock, he found himself sitting in his Herman Miller chair listening to Chopin reading something from the 19th century. Less frequently, he would have a visitor.

Beth had taken to materializing on what had become her favorite piece of furniture, the blue loveseat.

"What's that you're listening to?"

She didn't startle him anymore. Percy was at peace with her visitations. He had convinced himself that his grief over losing his parents had manifested itself in these visions, which, although troubling, were ultimately harmless. The fact that they were becoming less frequent only served to confirm his self-diagnosis. Besides, Beth's apparition had been transformed into something very much like a friend. Sam seemed to ignore Percy's dream visitor, and Beth had never made mention of him until tonight.

"That's Chopin, I think. You look nice tonight."

Beth looked very nice indeed in her tight black jeans, soft yellow chiffon sweater and pearls. Each appearance had her in a new outfit. This particular stage of grief had an exquisite sense of fashion.

"It's beautiful, whoever it is. So I see you finally got a dog. Oh, and thanks for noticing."

"I had basically given up on the search. There's a lot involved in getting a dog, lots of decisions to make. I didn't want to rush into anything. Then Sam here just showed up in the back yard."

"Wow. If you had done that much research before marrying me, you could have saved yourself a lot of trouble."

Percy felt oddly hurt by her remark. She was right, of course. After the encounter in Atlantic City, he had fallen so helplessly in love he was incapable of rational thought. His decision to marry Beth was made despite the protests of both of his parents, most of his colleagues, and every one of his female friends. The only votes in favor were from the guys on his softball team, who all professed shock that he had managed to snag a woman as smoking hot as Beth. If he had been afforded 30 minutes of contemplation, unencumbered by passion, he would have seen what everyone else saw, that Beth was as far removed from the world of Percy Hope as Paris was from Peoria. The Hopes were a steady tribe, multiple generations of clock punchers, with an occasional horse thief thrown in for color. Beth was everything he was not. She was hype to his calm. His personality of understated steadiness was almost comical next to her dazzling flamboyance. The match was made a considerable distance away from heaven, and yet her words had wounded him.

"It might have saved me a lot of trouble, but I would have missed out on a lot of fun."

"Not to mention some great sex."

"That too."

Beth rose from the loveseat and picked up a picture of Gilbert and Frances from the lamp table in front of the window.

"It might have been different if they would have accepted me."

"They tried to Beth; you just made it too hard. It's like you enjoyed provoking them, you enjoyed doing things that you knew would embarrass them."

"Guilty as charged. Maybe there was a part of me that wouldn't have been able to handle it if they fell in love with me too."

Beth turned to Percy. Her face was sad, full of regret, and she seemed to be fighting back tears. Then she blew him a kiss and vanished.

For Percy, these were the worst of times. Beth's appearances were becoming draped in regret and melancholy. She had transformed herself into a sympathetic character. After seeing her discomfort, after watching the weariness in her eyes, she became the woman he had fallen in love with, not the woman who almost destroyed him. She would disappear, and Percy would be left alone in his parents' house, trying to come to grips with the decisions he had made. He wanted the visions to end, but not too soon. He wondered, often late into the night, whether he should call her, make contact with flesh and blood Beth, but he never could summon the courage.

Percy turned off the music and sat in silence for a while. He always worried about his sanity after these encounters. How firm was his grasp on reality? The tidy explanations about stages of grief that he told himself the next morning seemed like self-delusion when he could still smell the perfume. He had thought about seeing Dr. Kennedy, the therapist who had actually done him some good after his collapse. She would probably have a more reliable clinical explanation for the visions.

He turned off the desk light and walked into the bathroom across the hall. As he brushed his teeth, he looked at himself in the mirror. Despite everything he had endured, he still looked young. His black hair still had no grey and was as thick as ever. His eyes were clear and reasonably energetic. In a suit and tie he could pass for handsome if graded on a curve. He wasn't grievously ugly, just something short of interesting. It took some external delight, some animating force to deliver him from ordinary. Beth. He had never thought of himself as more handsome than the times when he walked into a casino with her on his arm. He opened the medicine cabinet and reached for his Lexapro when he noticed it leaning against the Barbasol. It was a business card, one of Beth's old ones from when she sold real estate. "Beth Hope, Realtor." He never remembered seeing it before. He had shaved that very morning and never saw it. He flipped it over and Beth's delicate handwriting was clear... "Dinner at Harry's, Friday night, 7 o'clock. Please come." No telling how long that card had been in there. He had been eating Friday night dinners at Harry's for years now. At the same time, he couldn't remember her ever writing a message like this on one of her business cards before. They would have both been there together anyway when she worked for ReMax.

He threw the card in the trash, walked into the junk room, climbed into bed and stared at the ceiling for an hour. He would call Dr. Kennedy in the morning.

Harry's was a jewel. It was part casual bar, part fine dining, and part tranquil retreat. There was no "Harry." That was just the name that the real owner, Billy Foster, had chosen because it had sounded like a place he would have wanted to eat. Billy could never decide exactly what sort of place he wanted, so he divided it up into sections, each with a unique identity. Whenever Percy wanted a fine steak dinner, it was Harry's. Whenever he felt like a beer and some conversation, Harry's. On the rare occasion when he just wanted to smoke a cigar and read a good book without being bothered, he would head for the dark paneled smoking room in the back with the soft leather chairs. Eventually it had become his Friday night dinner spot, regardless of his mood. Harry's was the most comfortable place in Percy's increasingly uncomfortable world.

He entered around 6:45 and caught Billy's eye. "Percy Hope, my very best customer, without whom I would have been forced to close years ago!"

Billy had mastered the fine art of flattery, and along with his photographic ability to remember names, had a way of making everyone who entered his restaurant feel special. Despite the practiced tone, he managed to pull off sincerity. But tonight he looked concerned and pulled Percy to the side and began to whisper.

"Percy, I'm afraid your regular table is taken at the moment. My greeter is new and didn't know. I'm terribly sorry."

"That's ok Billy. I can sit anywhere."

"No, you don't understand. It's Beth."

Percy looked over Billy's right shoulder and saw the back of Beth's head, her shining red hair falling across the yellow chiffon sweater she was wearing when she last visited. Percy could feel his heart beating. For an instant he was sure that he should leave before she saw him.

"It's alright Billy. I'm fine. Let me go say hi, then I'll take a seat at the bar."

Percy walked slowly and quietly on the shining parquet floor until he reached her table. Beth looked up at him and smiled knowingly. "Hello, Percy. I knew you would come."

"I suppose I am nothing if not predictable, been eating at the same table in the same restaurant every Friday night for what, ten years?"

"You know what I mean." Beth was different somehow, quiet, subdued, almost meek. "Would it be asking too much for you to join me? Eating alone isn't much fun."

"Sure." The word came out without effort and without thought. He knew that he couldn't say no. There was just too much history and too many unanswered questions. He pulled out the chair across from her and signaled to Billy for a waiter. In an instant, the air seemed to rush out of the room, background chatter, the sounds of forks and knives against porcelain all sucked out of the place through the doors and windows, with nothing but Beth in slow motion across the table from him, smiling wildly. Percy recognized the leopard print dress, the short haircut, and now, the excited laugh that always followed her second vodka martini.

"Listen, we need to talk about something, and if I don't start now, I'm going to lose my nerve," he heard himself say.

"Before you start, I have something that I need to talk to YOU about." Beth was playful, exuberant, her eyes flashing with color. "Percy Hope, would you do me the honor of becoming my husband?"

The familiar sound of Harry's returned, and Percy looked

at an older, sadder Beth as she stirred the ice in her drink in front of him.

"When I first sat down, I couldn't help thinking about all the dinners we've eaten together at this very spot." She looked through the beveled glass window into the parking lot. "I remember one night in particular, the night I asked you to marry me."

Percy began to feel nervous, shaken by her tone and the confounding power she still possessed to read his mind. It was times like these that made Percy wonder if she also had the power to control his thoughts, some sort of supernatural power of suggestion.

"The first of a thousand times that you beat me to the punch."

"Do you think we were a mistake, Percy?"

"Yes."

She seemed disappointed, but not surprised at the answer. Something was wrong with her. The Beth he knew had an amazing ability to hold a gaze until hell froze over before looking away. It was unsettling to those who didn't know her, even uncomfortable to those who did. But since he had sat down, she had alternated between the window, her hands, and the menu with only quick, nervous glances at his eyes. Something was clearly wrong.

"Did you like my cake?"

It had been over a month since she had dropped off the pound cake after the funeral. It had been a strange ten-minute encounter, the first time she had entered the house in years. The conversation had been awkward, and as soon as she had left, Percy had jammed the cake, chunk by chunk, down the disposal. "Yes, it was quite good," he lied.

"Sure you didn't jam it down the disposal in a rage?"

Infuriating. "Why can't you just let me lie once in a while?"

"Ever since that night, you've been appearing in my dreams, Percy, almost every night."

◇ 5 ◇

"Finally, the key to your heart."

Sheila Kennedy sat in a brown leather wing-backed chair, scribbling discreetly in a notebook with a Montblanc pen. She was the only person alive who knew Percy's story, every messy detail. No matter the subject, her chilled, professional face never flinched. Not one trace of revulsion, shock, or even mild disapproval ever registered in her dark brown eyes. It had been several months since their last meeting. After a brief summary of the events leading up to and the aftermath of his parents' deaths, he got to the point.

"Beth brought over a cake a week or so after the funeral. It was very weird seeing her in the house. We hardly said a word, it was so awkward. I suppose she was making a gesture of some sort. Anyway, after that short visit, she has been appearing in my dreams. They're not really dreams, more like visions. I'll be minding my own business, and she will just appear out of thin air."

"Does she speak?"

"At first, no, but recently, we've been having regular conversations."

"What about?"

"Regrets, mostly. She seems contrite, like she wants to make amends somehow. But the real reason I'm here is that last Friday night I ran into her at Harry's. She was sitting at our table, waiting for me, really. She told me that ever since the day she brought over the cake, she too has been having vivid dreams... about me."

The unflappable doctor leaned forward ever so slightly, removing her reading glasses. "Really?" For Sheila Kennedy, this was akin to the reaction that a longshoreman might have had upon discovering that his foreman was gay. "How did this discovery make you feel?"

Although she had been of vital assistance to him in regaining his emotional footing after the breakdown, this was a particularly annoying part of the process. The "how does that make you feel?" routine, a staple of Kennedy's repertoire, always made Percy feel like he was being ripped off and short-changed. For $100 an hour shouldn't she be answering the questions?

"How do you think it made me feel?!" Percy rarely became angry with her, and the sudden outburst surprised him. "It freaked me out! I'm seeing my ex-wife appear as lifelike as you are right now practically every night, then she tells me that the same thing is happening to her? How would you feel, Doctor? And if you say something like, 'intrigued,' I'm leaving!"

"I'm sorry Percy. I suppose what I meant to ask was, with her history of reading your mind, did you feel that this admission by Beth was honest, or just something she said to rattle you?"

Sometimes Percy became so disappointed with himself, so ashamed of his naiveté, so appalled at his inability to comprehend the obvious that he would retreat into bouts of self-loathing that could immobilize him for weeks. Beth was playing him, again, picking at the scab of his emotional fragility.

Why could he not see it for himself? Why did he need a shrink to do his thinking for him?

"You say that these visions occur mostly at night, at your parents' house?"

"It's my house now, Dr. Kennedy, and yes she always appears at my house."

"Nowhere else? Never in the daytime?"

"No, just at night."

"Didn't the two of you live in... what was then your parents' house... for a couple of months early on in your marriage, when your house was being built?"

"It was actually only four weeks."

"So, does she still have a key?"

"What, are you suggesting that she's letting herself in every night and then disappearing into thin air?! She's not THAT good."

"I'm suggesting nothing of the sort. I just asked you if she still had a key."

"I guess she does. I don't remember getting it back from her, and honestly, I'm not even sure that I gave her one in the first place. What difference does it make?"

"Maybe no difference at all. But she only appears at the house, at night. I'm just thinking it through."

The session was over, and as usual, Percy had much to ponder. He drove the pickup around for an hour or so trying to sort everything out. He took the long way back, driving out into the farmland that surrounded the town that had been his home for 37 years. He had never owned a truck before and would never have been caught dead buying one, but he had become enamored with this one, the strangest part of his inheritance. He wondered why his father had replaced that tiny old Datsun with this monstrosity in the first place. He told himself he should sell it and use the money to buy something more suitable. It got terrible mileage, was way too high off the ground, and he often felt silly jumping up on the running board to get in the thing. There was just something about it that seemed right. He felt that it connected him with his father, that Gilbert would have been happy to know that he kept it, and proud to see him driving it around town. It was not without its comforts. The leather seating was luxurious, the interior design as good as most German sedans of 20 years ago, the sound system surprisingly good. Percy enjoyed the quirky pleasure of hearing Beethoven pulsing through the speakers of a monster truck. Sam was never happier and more content than when he rode shotgun with his tongue lapping wildly in the wind out of the passenger window.

The rolling hills always calmed him. Field after field of corn and soybeans looking perfectly ordered, expertly designed and cultivated calmed his nerves. The road narrowed and began to twist and turn as he got closer to the river. A heavily shaded picnic area on the right was empty. He pulled in, shut the engine and waited while Beethoven's piano sonata #21 finished in a manic crash of notes. Then, Percy jumped down from his soft leather seat onto the gravel parking lot and walked slowly out onto the bridge to the very spot where he had stood five summers ago. The water was grey and swirled in circles as it passed under the bridge. He had fished here as a child, swam in the cold, deep water when he was in high school, and had tried to kill himself by jumping in on a rainy night two days after his 32nd birthday. But Percy had a long history of beating the house, and instead of dead, he ended up unconscious, twisted up in the branches of a fallen oak tree barely 50 feet down river from the bridge. But today, he just looked at the water passing out of sight beneath him and thought of Beth, and Sheila Kennedy, and the green plastic that covered the two keys that Gilbert had given to him the night he and Beth had moved in, and the crazy laugh that she had unleashed when he placed one of them in her hand. "Finally, the key to your heart," she had said right before deciding to plant a long and inappropriately passionate kiss on him in front of both parents.

Thus had begun the four craziest weeks of his life. Percy had hoped that Beth would bond with his parents, his mother particularly, and there had been times of harmony and promise, but every night Beth had insisted on bouts of noisy, riotous sex. Before this, she had not been much of a talker during sex. Now suddenly she wouldn't shut up. Although Percy had been mortified at first, he couldn't summon the will to fight her off, since these four weeks would prove to be the best sex of his entire life. Nothing he had conjured up in even the wildest teenage dreams in this room prepared him for the unbridled sexual frenzy that Beth had unleashed on the small full size bed just down the hall from where his very old fashioned 70-year-old parents were trying to fall asleep. The first morning at breakfast, Gilbert and Frances looked stunned, perhaps surprised that Beth had survived what must have sounded to them like some sort of violent attack by a deadly animal. What little eye contact that was made was Frances glancing at Beth's arms for signs of cuts or bruises. Beth thoroughly enjoyed their discomfort, and even made remarks calculated for maximum embarrassment. "This son of yours has made me a happy woman, Frances, a VERY happy woman. I guess I owe it all to you!"

It was always a very mixed bag with Beth. To Percy, she was the most desirable human being in the universe, the most exhilarating presence, the essence of every earthly desire. He longed for her. She dominated his thoughts, and lived in his daydreams. Nothing made him more proud of himself than the knowledge that she had chosen him. And yet, there was an alien corner of her mind, a foreign shore on her soul. There was a curious mean streak, a sense of humor too heavily reliant on humiliation, too dependent on a foil. Her playfulness too often had a victim. Percy knew it, had watched it grow in their time together. It troubled him, but he knew that he could never walk away.

The long road finally led back to 16 Jennings Lane. He parked the truck under the carport awning and reached for the screen door at the top of the steps when he saw a plain white envelope stuck right above the handle. Inside was a bronze key coated at the top in green plastic.

◆ **6** ◆

The Borgata

Beth Harrison's life had always been about exceeding expectations. She had made a habit of beating the odds, of overcoming the very bad hand she had been dealt at birth. Child of a hooker, and ward of the foster care system would always dominate her life's early resume. Her existence had been a series of arranged relationships, first with several foster families and then the oddest arranged association of all – her acceptance into the University of Maryland. This had been a result of a give-a-poor-kid-a-shot welfare scheme doled out to a few students a year who tested well and showed intellectual promise. Beth had always assumed that any brain power she possessed must have come from her long ago forgotten father, the shadow from her memory who would come around once every couple of years when she was very young. It couldn't possibly have come from her hot mess of a mother who might have meant well but had so far demonstrated no discernible intellectual ability. Whoever she had gotten it from, her smarts had been her ticket out of a doomed life.

Once she arrived on the Maryland campus, she took full advantage of every opportunity presented to her. Her beauty opened doors, her brain did the rest. Although she quickly made friends, she learned early on how to conjure a believable story on a dime when one was needed. She invented an impressive family support system, knowing that her new sorority sisters couldn't tolerate the ugly truth. Conveniently, her parents lived across the country near Denver, Colorado, but spent much of their time traveling in Europe, which explained their absence during parents' weekends. Either her story was so perfectly believable that none of her friends bothered to check out the particulars, or she was so well liked and her company so charming that everyone believed the story because they wanted it all to be true. Although Beth had made many friends in her first years as an undergraduate, she had been under no illusions about the future. As soon as she graduated, she knew that she would never see any of them again. She had bigger fish to fry and new stories to invent.

Her first visit to a casino was the Borgata in Atlantic City. The instant she walked through the doors, she felt a surge of energy, a wild expectation. The sounds, the lights, the electric commotion, all appealed to her in a frenzied way. She walked slowly, wide-eyed, gawking at the extravaganza of it all, stumbling into people like a hick from the mountains. This was going to be one hell of a fun weekend. When Katherine Miller had asked her to be a bridesmaid, she had said yes out of obligation, and had regretted it ever since. Weddings just weren't her thing, so much fuss and bother over something that had a slim chance of success. How could one person possibly commit to another for all of eternity? It was all a Disney trap. But this, this place, this weekend, might just make it all worthwhile. Within 30 minutes she found herself at the bar throwing back drinks and flirting with a guy who spun the roulette wheel down the street at Harrah's.

"Bachelorette party, eh? You picked a great spot for one. Lucky for you, it's my day off, so I'll be glad to show you around, give you a few insider tips."

"Insider tips? What, how to pick up girls?" Beth was already tired of the guy. He talked too much and had managed to bore her in less than ten minutes, a new record.

Suddenly he looked over her shoulder and sat down with his drink. "Hey Rick," he yelled at his buddy down the bar, "look who just walked in!"

Rick looked over towards the lobby chandelier at the main entrance. "Holy crap! It's God!"

"Wait, God gambles?" Beth was starting to feel the drinks. "Where is God? I've always wanted to meet him."

"We just call him God, although sometimes man, I wonder. See that dude over underneath the chandelier wearing the Virginia sweatshirt? That is the luckiest man in America."

Rick had joined them and started with the stories. "He comes to town about once a month and plays everything, at several casinos, and wins almost everything he touches. He's always alone, and always stops when he's ahead, and he's always ahead. This city is like his ATM. But the craziest thing is, he always stops when he's up 20, 25 grand. He walks away. Damndest thing I ever saw."

"One time over at Harrah's, I saw him lay down four straight bets on 19 at my wheel. Won all four! Hell, before that night I had never spun the same number three times in a row, but God here, he cleans me for 10K betting four straight 19s. As soon as the suits start getting uncomfortable, he'll lose for a while, start doing dumb stuff like asking for another card sitting on 18 at blackjack or something like that. If he's cheating, nobody can prove it. He's got a gift, baby... he's God."

Beth was mesmerized. God was kind of cute. She grabbed her drink, left the bar, and began following the Virginia sweatshirt around at a safe distance. She liked his walk, its unhurried grace. She had always liked black hair, and he had a head full. He looked fit, probably worked out. Even without the Midas touch, he had appeal. She wondered why he was always alone.

After a few minutes he made his way to the roulette table. Beth hid behind a column and watched him lay several chips on number 22. Win. Next, he moved a larger stack to number 5. Win. Then he gathered his chips and left the table. What a beautiful man. The rest of the girls finally came down from their rooms all at once and found Beth. They distracted her for just a second, then, he was gone.

Later that night, after dinner, everyone was drunk and happy. It was time for Katherine to parade around with a tiara, losing money. Beth guided them all to the roulette table where she had last seen God. After a few minutes she spotted him trying to look inconspicuous behind a column. He was staring at her and the prospect of meeting him gave her a thrill. She was going to have to make a move somehow. If he disappeared again, she might never find him. Someone at the table cracked a raunchy joke about the queen needing a hot knight or something, and amidst all the laughter, Beth stared right into his eyes and hung on for dear life. The connection seemed magical. The next night they had dinner and talked about life. He was intelligent, a thinker, and nothing at all what Beth was used to in a man. By the time she had watched him win at blackjack three hours later that night, she had made the decision that he belonged to her.

She had hoped that seeing him at Harry's would have settled her nerves a bit, but it hadn't. Going there had been a mistake, too many memories. Where had she gotten the idea that he could possibly have forgiven her? She drove back to her lovely brick home, the largest jewel her lawyer had secured for her from the divorce. The house was ridiculously large, even when they were together, but now she rattled around in the place like a ghost. Sometimes at night her crying would produce an echo, but ever since Percy's appearances, she cried less often.

Her life had been transformed into a tortuous season of regret. The day that her divorce had been final, she had gotten everything she had wanted. The house was hers, the Mercedes, half of what was left of their investments. She had secured a respectable future and was finally free from him and his bleeding heart. The marriage had really ended when Percy made the decision to quit gambling. Beth never could accept what she considered such a scandalous waste. It had been a childish decision based on nothing more than misplaced guilt and some twisted notion of fairness. The divorce had been inevitable.

Beth had never had a close relationship with guilt. Guilt was about regret, and regret was a useless gesture. The past was the past, gone forever. The less said or done about it the better. Life was about today. Her first encounter with guilt had been as a child when her mother had dropped her off at a weeklong summer church thing called vacation bible school. It was the only church Beth had ever attended. For the entire week she had loved it. There were fun crafts and delicious snacks, and most of the other kids were nice. The ladies that ran the place seemed sweet and attentive. It was about the best experience of her young life right up until the final night when one of the speakers began talking of sin and guilt and the punishment that awaited her in hell if she didn't accept Christ as her savior. It had terrified her and confirmed in her young mind what her mother had always told her, "*Anything that seems good always has a hook in it.*" Her most recent encounter with guilt had been the day that Frances had called to tell her that Percy had lost everything over four days and nights in Vegas. It was his first visit to a casino in four years. He had wanted to win her back and was hoping a big win would change her mind about their future. His luck was gone, and he had lost it all.

She had cried when she hung up the phone. It was all so tragic. She had driven him to ruin, there wasn't a doubt in her mind. There were a few days of grief and guilt, but soon, she became angry. His foolish decision to give up his gift had resulted in its loss, and he had no one to blame but himself. He was broke? Then he could go back and live with his parents. It was none of her business. They weren't married any longer, to hell with him.

Then, a few weeks later, she got the call from Frances at the hospital. Percy had been pulled out of the river after trying to kill himself. He was going to make it, but Frances thought she should hear it from them before she read it in the papers. It was this horrible news from which she had never fully recovered. As horrified as she had been at the news, she couldn't bring herself to visit him at the hospital. The weight of her guilt was overpowering, crushing every hope and dream that she still possessed. The day that Percy was released from the hospital was particularly unsettling. All day she had thought of going to visit, or at least making an appearance at the house, saying something comforting to Frances, but she never could manage even a phone call. Her lack of courage, her inability to just this once overcome her fears and do the right thing, to just this once conquer her pride, to admit to her multiple shortcomings as a human being, had reduced her to thoughts of her own suicide.

Shortly after hanging up the phone, she had poured herself a drink and collapsed on the Queen Anne loveseat at the foot of her king-sized rice carved poster bed. She drew her knees up tightly to her chest and began to cry, silent tears streaming down her face in the darkness. Eventually she dozed off and slept awkwardly for an hour or so. When she awoke, the moon had risen, casting silver streams of moonlight across the floor. Still in jeans and a silk blouse, she got up and started towards the bed when she noticed a shining pool of water, illuminated by a moonbeam, slowly expanding its way out from under her closet door. Half asleep, she wondered at first whether it was just an odd reflection of some sort, a moonlight-induced optical illusion. She stood still for a moment and watched the pool slowly expand. Her drink, it must have been her drink. It probably had fallen out of her hand from the loveseat when she fell asleep. There, sure enough, was the thick glass on the floor not far from the closet door.

As she reached down to pick it up, she heard the tinny screech of the closet door hinge. She slowly stood and watched the door swing open, casting a shadow across the floor. There stood Percy, soaked through, his face ashen white, his eyes wide in horror, his arms twisted through the rotted limb of an oak tree. Beth let out a primal scream as she dropped the heavy glass onto the polished wood floor, where it shattered, sending slivers of glass scattering through the water, reflections from the moonlight lighting the floor up like crystal fireworks. The awful sound of her screams echoed through the great house and filtered back up the stairs, waking her bolt-upright in the bed. Her blouse was soaked through with sweat, the bed linens crumpled up in a ball in her fists. The sudden realization that it was just a dream produced even deeper wails of despair. Eventually, pure exhaustion dried up the tears. It was four in the morning and she rose to pour herself a drink. When she took a second step, a jagged shard of glass sliced a gash into her heel.

◇ 7 ◇

Unequally Yoked

Beth had no idea what had possessed her to make a pound cake in the first place. She wasn't a particularly good cook. Maybe she made it because it had been the only thing that Frances and she had ever done together, that gorgeous spring day forever ago when Frances had asked if she wanted to help her make a pound cake for a church covered dish supper. They had spent an enjoyable few hours in the kitchen chatting and laughing, Beth's one and only good day as a daughter-in-law. So her crazy notion had blossomed into an action, and before she had thought it through, there she was standing inside the front door, pawing the floor like a nervous school girl, hoping that Percy would soften a little and ask her to stay for coffee. Instead, Percy looked cold and agitated at her presence inside his house, his parents' house, on the very spot where she had stood looking so radiant 12 years ago.

So she smiled, and touched his hand briefly while telling him that he was in her prayers, as she walked back through the door.

"Since when?" Percy had said in a voice chilly with resentment. "You've never said a prayer in your life."

Beth stopped half way down the front steps and turned to look at him through the screen. "I just picked it up a few months ago, trying to make a few changes." As she backed the Mercedes out of the driveway, Percy was still standing there, watching her leave.

On the drive home, Beth wondered what must have been going through Percy's mind at the very idea that she was capable of saying a prayer at all, much less for him! Beth had always been a rather loud atheist. It had been one of the many objections that Frances had made to Percy when the news of marriage broke through the Hope home. Frances had looked her straight in the eye. "If you marry my son, you will be unequally yoked together."

A curious expression enveloped Beth's face, and before she could stop herself, she had heard herself say, "What the hell? Are we a team of mules? Do I look like an ox to you? What on earth are you talking about?"

Beth had never been able to come to grips with the Hope family religion, and to make it worse, could never even talk about it without falling into sarcasm and the soft insults of condescension. So, eventually, the subject was dropped. In all of their married life, their one and only appearance in church had been their wedding day.

Now, 12 years and a tidal wave of sin later, Beth had, out of personal desperation, taken a few tentative steps towards reacquainting herself with the Christian God. It had started bizarrely enough. She had found herself in a hotel lobby talking to a very handsome man in a fabulous suit, wondering what he would be like in bed when he began to talk about religion. Instead of boring her to tears, he had seemed intelligent, interesting and sincere, traits she didn't associate with religion. Before he left, he had reached into his briefcase, pulled out a worn out paperback book and given it to her as a parting gift. Somebody named G.K. Chesterton (who from the photograph on the back was a dead ringer for Orson Welles) had written a book called The Everlasting Man, and this hand-some, successful man had given it to her with the admonition to read it with an open mind and let the chips fall where they may. So she had. She didn't understand half of it, but what she did understand captivated her. From there she had picked up Mere Christianity by C.S. Lewis. Everything was so new, and there was much she couldn't accept, but the one newfound concept that had overwhelmed her, transformed her was the Christian notion of grace. While Beth still wouldn't be caught dead inside a church, the stories about forgiveness and grace gave her a glimmer of hope, that there was at least an infinitesimal chance at redemption for what had become her train wreck of a life.

As she drove home in the dying sunlight after the pound cake debacle, she knew she was in for another long and lonely night. She made herself a western omelet and a couple of pieces of cinnamon toast, a habit she had picked up while married to Percy, breakfast for dinner. Then she walked through the French doors off the living room into the book-lined walls of the study that Percy had insisted on placing in this partic-ular spot so he could share the living room fireplace. It had cost them a fortune to have a double fireplace, but Percy had always wanted to be able to read his books beside a roaring fire. Besides, back then, money hadn't really been an issue, so here it was, the most tastefully decorated and least used room in the house.

Lately, Beth had started to come in after dinner, after getting ready for bed. She would sit at his old desk and read through one of the strange new books she had been intro-duced to by the man in the fabulous suit. Tonight it would be The God Who Is There by Frances Schaeffer. But tonight the room was unusually dark. The blinds had been closed. She hadn't remembered doing it, so it must have been her new Bolivian maid, Maria. She reached for the light switch, flipped it on, then walked behind the solid oak desk to open the blinds because, even though it was dark outside, closed blinds felt creepy. When she turned around to pull the leather desk chair out, she saw Percy sitting in his old Shaker rocking chair by the fireplace. She let out a girlish scream, high-pitched and delicate, as she covered her mouth with both hands. He was wearing soft blue seersucker pants, a white polo shirt, and a pair of topsiders with no socks. He said nothing, just looked directly into her eyes with an expressionless face. Beth gathered herself, wondering how he had gotten into the house. Had she left the front door unlocked? The last time she had seen him in the house was during that awful nightmare the night he had tried to kill himself. Maybe this was just another dream, an indigestion problem. Who eats a western omelet at nine o'clock at night anyway? Served her right.

"I find this considerably difficult to believe, Beth," he spoke. Sounded like Percy. He looked and sounded so real. The only thing that looked wrong was the clothes. Seersucker?

"Yeah, well, I'm having a hard time believing this too," she heard herself say in a surprisingly calm voice. Then she noticed the books in his lap.

"Chesterton, Lewis, Schaeffer? What's gotten into you? Mom could have died a happy woman had she lived long enough to see this."

"Don't get too excited. I don't understand half of it, and I have trouble believing the half I do understand, just trying to broaden my horizons."

"Bullshit."

"How did you get in here?"

"Walked right through the walls, dear. Where else would I go dressed like this?"

Beth's heart rate had begun to drop, and her breathing was back to normal. She slowly sat down and heard the irritating squeak of the chair.

"You need to WD-40 that. I'd do it for you, but I don't live here anymore, remember?"

"Why did you say bullshit?"

"See, one great thing about being in a dream, being an imagined thing, is that you get to say whatever you want. When you hear bullshit, you get to call it out. I think you're reading those books because you feel guilty for being such a pathetic excuse for a wife, and really a pathetic excuse for a human being all these years. So, you've latched on to faith as a way to assuage your guilt, to beat back your well-earned despair."

Beth looked away for the first time and absorbed the intensity of his words. They rolled over her, a tsunami of truth, drowning her in guilt. The real Percy would have had enough class to spare her the humiliation. The real Percy would have avoided this sort of airing of grievances, this sort of emotional confrontation.

"I think 'pathetic' is pretty harsh. 'Disappointing' would be better. It would allow me to hang on to at least a shred of self-respect."

"Fair enough." Percy stood up and walked over to the French doors. "I can accept 'disappointing.'"

Beth noticed that his feet hovered just above the floor; his skin had become softly translucent, as if he was preparing to evaporate, to leave her alone in the big house. She stood up and took a step toward him. "Percy, do you think that there is even the smallest chance that you could ever bring yourself to forgive me?"

"I'm a dream, Beth. Forgiveness is for the living." He walked through the French doors and vanished.

◇ **8** ◇

Shacklefords' Finest

Percy removed the key from the envelope and laid it on the kitchen counter, his mind racing. Everything with Beth had about it the scent of the supernatural, from the mind reading to the late night appearances, to her almost impossible beauty. It was all so exhausting. He needed a beer. There was one left in the refrigerator. He reached into the cabinet for a glass. They all must have been in the dishwasher, which hadn't been run. Behind an old pewter German stein was a tall, clean glass with a worn out label... Schlitz. It had been Gilbert's favorite.

Percy sat back down, poured the beer straight into the bottom of the glass so a thick stand of foam would rise to the top like his dad used to do. It was funny how things worked out, thought Percy. It had only been a week after he had gotten his head screwed back on straight, just a week after his last session with Kennedy when Gilbert had his stroke. If it had happened six months earlier, Percy would have been absolutely no help to his mother. As it turned out, caring for his dad had given him a project, something outside of himself to focus on, a chance to be a good son.

The stroke had been massive, taking with it Gilbert's

47

ability to walk, speak, or control his bowels. The daily care requirements were overwhelming, but Frances wouldn't even consider some sort of nursing home or assisted living facility, as she viewed anything other than sitting at his bedside 24 hours a day to be a betrayal. But she was too weak to lift him, bathe, or feed him. It had fallen to Percy, and he had taken up the job with great eagerness and enthusiasm. But the daily grind wore on him. He found that he was caring not just for his dad but for his rapidly declining mother. The burden was heavy, but he felt closer to his parents than he ever had before, and for nearly two years he had been so consumed with the work, his mind had finally managed to break free from Beth.

Still, it was devastating work. Watching his dad suffer the daily humiliations of incontinence, seeing the frustration in his eyes as he tried vainly to speak, sometimes it was all too much. Once he had gotten them both down for the night, Percy would often go outside, sit on the front steps and cry out to God in bitterness and rage. His father didn't deserve this, nobody did. Gilbert, a powerful man's man of legendary strength and integrity, had been reduced to wearing diapers and scratching out block letters on a notepad left-handed, one and two-word requests for this or that. But enduring the crucible of his parents' care had its small rewards. After one particularly horrible bowel accident, Percy had stripped the bed clothes, removed the soiled pajamas, given his dad a bath, and finally gotten him back in a clean bed, when he noticed tears coming from his dad's one good eye. "What's wrong Pop?" Gilbert had asked for his pencil and notepad and scribbled out, "good son" in shaky letters.

By the time he died that Tuesday morning in his sleep, he weighed 100 pounds. Frances, already weakened from the ordeal, and so devastated by his loss, was gone by seven o'clock that evening. They hadn't spent a day apart in 60 years, and tomorrow wouldn't be the first.

So, after two years of tender care and devotion, Percy lost

them both in one day and was suddenly, relentlessly... alone.

All of his life Percy had longed for a brother or sister, but never more than at the precise moment when he realized that arrangements had to be made to bury his parents and there was nowhere else to turn, no one to come alongside him and walk him through it, that he was the last surviving Hope, a family tree that would henceforth wither. He knew nothing about funerals or cemeteries, nothing of the business of death. A wife would have been nice, even an estranged one, but he couldn't bear the phone call. Ted and Beatrice Clark, next door neighbors for 22 years, would rescue him by finding a plot, while Percy would contend with the Shacklefords funeral home and its sharply dressed Bob Townsend, Shacklefords' most credentialed and celebrated mortician. Bob extended his hand, grasped Percy's elbow with the other, and got a little too close while sincerely whispering, "I am so, SO sorry for your loss."

Bob then led him into a dimly lit "counseling office," offered him something to drink, then crossed his hands soberly and looked into his eyes with the most excruciatingly earnest expression that Percy had ever encountered.

"Words cannot possibly express the depth of loss you must be feeling at this moment, the intensity of your grief, but at Shacklefords we pride ourselves on making the best out of bad situations."

Percy believed him. How could he not? His suit was dark and impeccably tailored; his hair parted in a perfect line, fastidiously groomed, his eyes tender with concern. He knew how awful this moment was. He felt it, professionally. This was his craft, his mission in life, to walk people through the valley of the shadow of death. Percy felt a deep gratitude for Bob Townsend.

Bob placed a thick stack of forms on the desk in front of him, and with a soft, whispered tone started with, "You will need to write an obituary. Since you teach college English, I'm sure you will do a fine job. I believe the standard length runs about $800."

"Wait." Percy wasn't sure he understood. "It cost $800 to place an obituary in the Times-Dispatch?"

Bob beamed a patient smile Percy's way. "For small local newspapers, obits are a vitally important profit center, without which they simply couldn't survive. Most people have no idea, so it's not surprising that you might be taken aback. You can always trim down your remarks to the basics... survived by, etc."

"Well there's just me now, no other family."

"Well then, problem solved." Bob Townsend was the solver of problems, and that most valuable of assets, an honest guide through a strange and unknown place. "Now, let's get the financial particulars out of the way first so we can concentrate on the service. Did your parents have life insurance?"

"Yes, several policies, in fact. But I haven't even begun to fill out that paperwork yet."

"Not a problem at all, Percy. May I call you Percy, or would you prefer Mr. Hope?"

"Percy is fine."

"So, how will you be paying for our service?"

"I'll just write you a check today, if that's alright. I have a Power of Attorney."

"Wonderful!" Bob seemed a bit too animated with the "wonderful," his voice rising an octave, as though he could hardly contain his excitement upon learning that Shacklefords would be paid today, up front. Briefly, Percy allowed himself to wonder how Bob was paid. Was he on salary, or did he receive a commission? It was a stray thought brought on by the visible lift in Bob's spirits once he had discovered that Percy was not indigent. "Now Percy, let's go back through the showroom, shall we?"

Wait. There was a showroom? Where could it be? All he had seen was what looked like the inside of a church and long hallways with deacon benches against the walls. Where could a showroom possibly be hiding, and what on earth would be in there?

Bob led Percy down a long hallway and opened a double door which led into a large, dimly lit room with rows upon rows of casket samples, short, sawed-off caskets illuminated with soft directional lights from on high. Every few feet there were potted plants and great, ponderous ferns hanging from the ceiling. Bob directed his attention to a beautifully polished mahogany box protruding from the wall at a provocative angle. "This is our finest casket, the Star Legacy Silver Tapestry 1000 with the very best all velvet interior, polished premium swing handles, sculpted corner, poly sealed, of course, and completely environmentally friendly."

"Yes, it's very nice." Environmentally friendly?

"Of course, all of our burial homes come with a limited one year warranty. But we have never had a product failure in the 45 years that we've been in business. Percy, I must say, this Star Legacy would do your beloved parents proud. When the guests arrive and see this fine product at the front of our chapel, they will instantly know how much you truly loved your folks."

"How much is it?" Only a limited warranty? Burial homes?

"Now again, this is our top-of-the-line product, and if you were to choose this, you would naturally want to go with the titanium-lined crypt. Yes, these crypts are six inches of steel-reinforced concrete with the finest liner in the industry, titanium, ensuring that your parents will not be disturbed by the elements for a century or more."

"Yes, that's good to know. How much is it?" Percy was starting to feel uncomfortable, similar to the way he felt whenever he bought a car.

"How long have your folks been married, Percy?" Bob placed his arm gently around Percy's shoulder and began steering him away from the Star Legacy and back towards the door.

"Um, a long time, uh, I can't really remember how many years actually."

"I'd say by their age, at least 55 years, wouldn't you say? Fifty-five years of marriage, now that's something you don't see much of anymore. And they were so close, so perfectly yoked together, that your dear mother couldn't face another day without him. You know, most folks wouldn't look at it this way, but I think that's terribly romantic, don't you?"

"I suppose..." Dying on the same day was anything but romantic, but Bob was the expert.

"And now, they will be united, in a manner of speaking, in death just as they were in life. Now, wouldn't you want their final resting place to be a place of class and dignity? That's why I guided you to the Star Legacy, Percy. Your parents were special, even their deaths were special. Our very best is really the only option for you."

By the time they were back in the counseling room and Bob had finally gotten around to telling him that Shacklefords' very best was going to cost $26,000, Percy just signed the papers without an objection. He just wanted for it to be over, so he could leave this tiny closet, say goodbye to Bob and leave this suffocating, poorly lit mausoleum.

Later that same day, the Clarks had come over the house to fill him in on the $18,000 worth of plots that they had managed to secure over at the Sheltering Arms cemetery. Beatrice had assured him that Gilbert and Frances' final resting place would be in the finest neighborhood in the place, not 40 feet away from the life-size statues of Jesus and his disciples, in what amounted to a (very) quiet cul-de-sac on Ascension Avenue. Percy thanked them both for helping out and then collapsed into a chair at the kitchen table. In one afternoon, he had managed to spend more than his parents spent in a year. The very last thing he wanted to do was go back to Shacklefords for a viewing and face 300 people. But, that was the correct protocol, and it had to be done. Percy would try to take a nap, then put on his best suit and head over to meet Bob at five o'clock.

The three hours of the viewing were the most difficult of Percy's life. He had not been prepared for the sight of his father and mother lying cold and still in their mahogany caskets, dressed for church, their skin powdered white, their mouths stitched together, their frail hands crossed piously as they lay snugly in their velvet tombs. Gilbert was skeletal, his cheeks sunken in on his jaws, hardly recognizable. Frances lay silent, her ashen cheeks slathered in makeup to give them color, her lips but thin purple lines cutting across her face. Percy had wanted to slam both lids shut on such a morbid spectacle! But Bob had been there to reassure him of the therapeutic benefits that open-caskets provided. He spoke of closure and peace, and as he did so, guided him away from them both to a large wing-backed chair a comfortable distance away. Then the people began to filter in. A serpentine receiving line formed out the viewing room door and down the hall, through the front door and down the sidewalk out front. Everyone was whispering, and greeting each other grimly, first walking past the caskets, then making their way around the display of flowers towards where Percy stood greeting them one by one.

Percy was gratified at the size of the crowd and what that said about his parents. There were people he hadn't seen in years, people who meant a lot to him, and several whose appearance had surprised him, some whom he didn't even know. Old ladies would greet him in tears with big tender hugs, telling stories of how much his folks had meant to them years before Percy had even been born. After the first two hours, Percy began to wilt under the heavy realization of just how alone and abandoned he truly had become. As each of his friends and colleagues paid their respects, Percy made mental notes of just how poor a job he had done at fashioning strong, secure friendships. Who among these hundreds of well wishers could he call next week just to go out for coffee and catch up without it seeming forced and awkward? There was no one.

About the time he had thought he couldn't handle another minute of the torture, he heard a hush fall over the already hushed crowd, and when he looked up, he saw her signing the guest register. It had been over a year, maybe longer, since he had seen her, and there she was, coming to pay her respects to her former in-laws. Something inside Percy broke. The tide of tears that had been rising for two days unabated broke through in a torrent. An audible gasp rippled through the room as Percy let out an agonizing groan, then a high-pitched, animal-like yelp. His body began to spasm and shake with the violence of his sobs. Beth ran to his side and got there just in time to keep him from falling to his knees. He melted into her arms and she began to cry with him. The gathered mourners covered their mouths with handkerchiefs and looked away. Bob slowly, quietly, expertly took command and thanked everyone for coming. The viewing was over.

Beth had also come to the funeral and sat beside him in the chapel. They spoke not a word the entire service. Then she had sat with him on tan folding chairs under the midnight blue Shacklefords tent at the graveside. They had front row seats as the caskets were lowered into the titanium-lined crypts. They saw the preacher toss handfuls of red clay in after them. After the last "amen," Percy and Beth tossed single roses into the great yawning pits and watched them bounce off the finely polished mahogany. Again, no words, just a parting hug. Percy watched her walk away in her elegant black dress, silky black gloves covering her arms up to the elbows. Without looking back, she got into his old Mercedes and drove away.

◇ **9** ◇

Guilt

After reading a succession of books that had both intrigued and baffled her, Beth had come to the conclusion that she probably needed to roll the dice on finding a church that she could attend anonymously where she might find answers to her many questions. Maybe there was someplace where she could slip in the back row and then be the first to leave, while wearing a disguise less anyone she knew might see her. She found a flier attached to a telephone pole outside her grocery store advertising a new kind of church for people who couldn't stand church. Sounded like her kind of place, so out of personal desperation, she had very cautiously started attending.

It turned out to be one of those beginner churches that had sprung up virtually overnight around town, the ones that met in middle school gyms at ten o'clock Sunday mornings, where the preacher wasn't called preacher or anything really, besides "Dave." You would walk in and everybody would be drinking coffee, walking around in khaki shorts and t-shirts. There would always be a band of some sort on a stage lit with colored lights. Most of the band members had long hair and tattoos. Most of the people were younger than the crowd Beth expected to find at church. The people were warm and welcoming and seemed utterly without guile, and every time she walked through the front doors it freaked her out a little, even after she had been attending off and on for three months. A random thought would flash through her mind on some Sundays... "What the hell am I doing here?"

Dave and his wife, Melinda, had taken a special interest in her, or at least it felt that way, since they would both make bee-lines towards her the second she walked in the place every week. At first it was creepy, but after getting to know them both a little, she looked forward to the attention, although Beth instinctively knew that no matter how many books she read, she would never learn how to be as sweet and tender-hearted as Melinda. Impossible.

After the service one Sunday, Beth had gone out for lunch with the two of them and had a long discussion about the concept of grace. Beth mostly listened as Dave laid it out for her, this mind-blowing New Testament idea, which seemed to Beth to be both simplistically naïve and powerfully transformational at the same time. After an hour or so, Melinda had promised to give her yet another book to read and, true to her word, had eventually produced a brand new paperback by somebody named Spurgeon entitled "All of Grace."

As she began to read, all she could think of was Percy. All of this religion and spirituality crap was going to be a worthless waste of time if she couldn't find a way to make peace with him. The one reality in Beth's life was the fundamental, foundational truth that she had used Percy. She had hitched her wagon to a gambling prodigy shooting star, had ridden him for all he was worth, and then dumped him when the money stopped flowing. She had treated him terribly, bankrupted him and driven him mad. The pain of her guilt and shame had been so consuming, it had driven her, against her better judgment, to risk public humiliation by showing up at the funeral home in a room full of his friends who rightly despised her for what she had done. As she stood in line in the dark hallway outside the viewing room, she could sense the tension, could feel the heat of their disapproval. When she entered the room, she caught a glimpse of him shaking an old lady's hand, and tears began to form in her eyes. She quickly hid behind a large man in a three piece suit, then saw the guest register on top of a wooden pulpit stand. She noticed that what little noise there had been in the room had become fainter still as she signed her name.

The loud, anguished groan startled her. She looked up from the register and saw Percy's pulsing red face contorted by an unspeakable loss, saw the hot tears streaming down his face, saw him beginning to fall, and all she knew to do was to run to him. She wrapped her arms around him and held him as tightly as she could as his body became wracked with spasms of grief, wave after wave, washing over him. By the time it was over, they were alone in the room except for Bob Townsend, who had the good sense not to rush them out. Beth wanted to tell him how much she cared for him, that she really had loved him, and in fact still loved him, but she didn't have the courage, couldn't conjure up the strength. So she just held him until he had gathered himself, until the tears were gone. The only words she managed to speak were barely above a whisper, and had about them the tone of an apology, "Percy, would you have any objection if I came to the funeral tomorrow? I don't want to be a distraction; I'll come late and sit in the back if that's ok."

"Don't be silly. Of course you can come. I would like that very much. Could you possibly sit with me? There's no one left in my family, as I'm sure you know."

And that was the extent of their entire conversation over a day and a half of being together after nearly two years apart. No words, just Beth holding on to Percy's trembling hands at the graveside. It had all been so strange, such a bizarre encounter, so ridiculously unfinished. The pound cake had been Beth's attempt at writing a better ending, or perhaps sparking a new beginning, neither of which had worked. Percy's coldness had startled her, nothing had really changed. The tenderness of heart at the funeral had just been a moment of crisis. Percy had recovered his hatred.

Beth sat in Percy's old leather chair, which occasionally still had his smell, and labored through the first chapter of the Spurgeon book. It was a strange book full of corny phrases. "Reader, do you mean business reading these pages?" She threw the book aside, spun around in the chair and looked out the window into the night. She had been waiting all day for the phone to ring, hoping he would call to ask about the key. Maybe, just maybe, it would have sparked a fond memory. She had stumbled across it in the bottom of the silverware drawer while looking for a corkscrew. Why had Gilbert had it coated in that weird green plastic? She remembered how happy it had made her that Gilbert had thought to make one for her, and when Percy had placed it in her hand she had been overcome with a delirious sensation, something close to joy, at the idea of being part of something, of being accepted into a family. It had been the moment when she had fallen in love with Percy, two years after walking down the aisle; better late than never. But the phone didn't ring. Would it ever ring?

The stars had become brighter each time she opened her eyes. The moon had slid down the horizon and turned the stage over to the lesser lights, when Beth saw Percy's reflection in the window. He was sitting in his rocking chair as he always was when he presented himself to her late at night. The seersucker had given way to jeans and a UVA Cavalier t-shirt, with that strange, uniquely irritating expression, "wahoowa," emblazoned across the front. He used to always wear that particular shirt just to piss her off, since she had graduated from the University of Maryland and had developed a healthy distaste for Mr. Jefferson's university.

"Never thought I would hear myself say that I missed

seersucker." Beth smiled warmly at her visitor. It always lifted her spirits to see him, real or imagined.

"Why did you return the key?" As usual, the Percy of her dreams was characteristically direct.

"I was digging through the silverware looking for my corkscrew, and there it was. I don't know why I gave it back really. It made me smile when I found it; it brought back some pretty sweet memories actually."

Percy had the key in his hands and looked up from it to examine Beth's eyes. A bemused look came over his face. "Sweet memories?"

"You wouldn't understand, and I'm not sure I could even explain it anyway, but yeah, good memories. So, I just thought I'd drop it off when I was over your way today."

"Bullshit."

"What? That's the truth."

"I'd be willing to bet my substantial inheritance that you made a special trip to drop off that key, hoping you would catch me at home. You can't bullshit a ghost, Beth."

Beth smiled and spun the chair around so she wouldn't have to face him as she said, "Ok. Alright, maybe I did make a special trip. What's so horrible about that?"

"The only memory that key brings up for me is the best four weeks of sex we ever had."

"I was in love with you, Percy, more in those four weeks than at any other time we were together."

"That's right, Beth. You were in love with me, right up until the day I stopped gambling. In sickness and in health, in poverty as well as wealth... except we were never poor, were we Beth? I won so much money we paid cash for the house and stashed enough money away to live a decent life. But that wasn't enough for you, was it Beth? But, hey, it's worked out pretty well for you, I must admit. You've got this great house, you're sitting at my old desk, driving my old car, and living off my old money, so... not bad."

"I'm a different person now, Percy. I'm not the same woman I was back then."

"Then, give it all back."

The next morning, two song birds stirred Beth awake along with the bright rays of summer sun streaming through the windows of the study. She lifted her head from the desk and felt the stiffness and pain in her neck and shoulders from sleeping at such an odd angle. Then she saw the golden reflection of the green plastic coated key on the seat of Percy's old rocking chair.

◆ **10** ◆

JoJo's Scar

Melinda Listrom had graduated from Baylor University then gone to some seminary in Texas to get a Master's in counseling, which is where she had met Dave. It had been a whirlwind romance, and within six months they were married. Now, four years later, they are broke, living in an apartment on the bad side of town, deliriously happy, trying to start a church from scratch. If Beth had searched the universe trying to find someone with whom she had less in common, she would never have found anyone better suited for the role than Melinda.

But today, Beth was on the clock, a patient, paying Melinda $50 an hour for something called "Christ-centered counseling." Beth sat across from Melinda in their cheaply decorated living room, sipping tea from fine china cups, which had been a wedding gift from Dave's grandmother. That piece of information had been offered apologetically by Melinda in an attempt to explain how a struggling minister's wife could afford something so elegant and refined. Beth thought it strange that she would feel the need to explain the presence of something so beautiful. There was so much about Christian people that Beth would never understand.

Although Melinda could be baffling at times, there was something so rare about her, so hard for Beth to fathom, this radiating sense of purpose, this all-encompassing contentment with her life just the way it was, this strange awareness that she was exactly where she was supposed to be, doing exactly what she was supposed to be doing. Melinda called it being in the "center of God's will." When Beth had asked how she could be so sure what God actually wanted, she had answered honestly and with a big beaming smile, "I can't explain it, and I know it sounds presumptuous, but I know, I just know." It was this sort of honesty that prompted Beth to trust her enough to tell her the wretched story of her life.

"Melinda, I'm here because I've read all the books you have given me. I've listened to all of Dave's sermons, and I've learned a lot, I really have. But the bottom line is, it's not doing me any good. I think I might be beyond redemption. I've lived the kind of life that produces casualties. My life is a bell that can't be unrung. I can't just put my past back in a bottle and start over."

Over the next three weeks, in five one-hour sessions, Beth spilled out the whole story. Melinda listened patiently, asked the occasional question, but basically just let her tell it her own way. The crux of Melinda's "Christ-centered advice" was saved for the very end. "Beth, your problem isn't that Percy won't forgive you. Your problem isn't even that God can't forgive you. Your problem is that you can't forgive yourself."

* * *

Percy had spent the better part of four hours grading some of the most ill-conceived, poorly-written freshman composition papers of his entire career and was in dire need of a drink. He looked at the bird clock on the wall and saw the mockingbird getting ready to sing, which meant it was eight o'clock in the evening. He truly hated the bird clock, but it was one of his mother's favorite things, and Percy hadn't had the heart to throw it out, so there it was hanging on the wall of his library. Every hour, on the hour, a different bird took a shot at announcing the passage of time. After 11 years most of them sounded like AM radio static. The mockingbird, the owl and the raven still had their pipes, so the hours of four, eight and midnight rang out loud and clear. With each strained sound that the clock made, Sam would let out a slow, menacing growl. Irritating as it was, it never failed to remind him of Frances and how much he missed her.

He walked into Harry's at 8:15 and took a seat at the bar. The rich, dark wood had a slick enamel coating that gave it a high gloss. Inlaid in the wood were random yellow blocks of diamond-shaped bamboo. Billy had spent a fortune, but it was the centerpiece of the entire place, and everyone had an opinion one way or the other. Percy loved it except for the bamboo diamonds, so he always sat directly in front of one so he could cover it with his drink napkin. Percy ordered vodka and grapefruit juice and sat it on the napkin. When he had been in college the drink used to be called a greyhound. Now, that seemed silly, so he always just asked for vodka and grapefruit juice so he didn't sound pretentious.

A month had gone by since the "passing," which is the word he had settled on to describe losing both of his parents on the same day. It sounded less horrible, less traumatic than it had actually been to live through, which made it the perfect word, elegant yet misleading, classy yet disingenuous, the perfect word. After finally learning how to live without Beth, or even the idea of Beth, the passing had brought her back into his life with a vengeance. She now was back on her throne, front and center of his every waking thought, and most of his non-waking ones. Suddenly she was everywhere. She shows up at the viewing, practically saves his life, and then shows up at the house with a cake, then in his dreams, so real he could almost taste her. Then she shows up at his table at Harry's, looking and sounding like a different woman than the one he married, or the one he had divorced.

The second drink tasted better than the first, the third better than the first two put together. Percy was feeling better about things and suddenly wanted company. It usually didn't take long at Harry's, Percy knew everybody who came in most nights. Soon someone would walk by, and Percy would strike up a conversation that would end up turning into a thought-vacation from Beth. To his great surprise, he found himself drunk. This wasn't Percy's modus operandi, and even though Billy, as usual, was running around the place like a chicken with his head cut off, he noticed and came over to investigate. "So are we celebrating or crying tonight?"

"WE are doing neither. WE are restocking our body's supply of Vitamin C."

Whenever Percy was drunk, every word that came out of his mouth became drenched in sarcasm that quickly turned venomous. Percy Hope was not a happy drunk.

"Well, you might want to pace yourself there, Percy."

But Billy had a restaurant to run, so Percy was left at the bar working on drink number five when a loud and merry party of eight entered the building. Percy looked towards the noise and saw him with an unlit cigar in his mouth, laughing entirely too loud. Percy no longer wished to be at the bar in Harry's, but if he had to be, he sure was glad to be drunk.

JoJo Sinclair always wore an expensive suit accentuated with one flourish after another, from loud silk tie to matching handkerchief, which always was bursting forth provocatively from his suit pocket. There was always some ostentatious display of jewelry, diamond cuff links or the latest fashion statement in watches. By careful design, he always looked rich. Joseph Johnston Sinclair was well off, ran a prosperous real estate company, but he wasn't nearly as rich as he looked, and everyone in town knew it. Everyone in town also knew that JoJo and Beth had had a "thing" while Beth was still Mrs. Beth Hope.

Percy turned his swivel bar stool so he could see the show, because with JoJo, entering any public place was always a show. He had been named after some old Civil War general who his mom claimed to have been related to, and perhaps she was right since JoJo always looked to be in command of something: big loud mouth, big loud car, and a big loud party of eight asking for a table. Percy watched him, watched his egotistical swagger, saw the hot blonde on his arm, and hoped that he could contain himself if JoJo saw him and came over for a chat. Percy couldn't keep his thoughts under control. Soon the images were clear and dancing in his head.

It had been an extraordinarily hot day. Percy was about to begin a lecture on Shakespeare's The Tempest when the room started spinning around. He steadied himself on the lectern until order had been restored, but by then he had begun to sweat profusely and was suddenly stricken with abdominal cramps. Class was abruptly canceled and Percy spent the next 15 minutes in the faculty lounge bathroom suffering absurd spasms of diarrhea. Whatever was wrong had come on him suddenly, and for the first time in his tenure at UVA, Percy missed a class because of illness.

He had driven home, hoping that his next spasm would at least do him the courtesy of waiting until he got there. He thought about calling Beth to let her know he was sick, but she would be home in a few hours anyhow, so he let it go. He made it through the front door and headed towards the kitchen to see if there was any Pepto-Bismol when he heard a faint murmur coming from his study. For a second he thought he had left the radio on, but then he heard what sounded like Beth's voice. She must have come home early. He opened the door to the study to tell her that he was sick and that she should keep her distance. Beth's red hair flowed down the smooth, perfect, whiter-than-white skin of her arching back. She was sitting on the naked lap of JoJo Sinclair, committing adultery with her boss in Percy's leather desk chair; both so rapturously engaged that neither was aware of his presence. After an agonizing moment of shock and the resulting indecision, Percy flew into a rage.

Beth screamed, jumped off of JoJo, and quickly grabbed at her clothes on the floor, Eve-like, suddenly ashamed of her nakedness. JoJo nearly flipped the chair over trying to cover himself. Percy quickly opened a drawer out of the built-in bookcases that lined the walls around the fireplace and pulled out an unloaded handgun that even Beth didn't know he owned and pointed it straight at JoJo's panic-stricken eyes. Beth screamed at the sudden escalation. JoJo began to plead with Percy to calm down, so that he could explain that this all wasn't what it looked like, exactly what all degenerate cheaters say in the movies right before their brains get blown out. Beth was crying and begging him to listen to reason when Percy ordered her out of the room. Then he began to cry himself. As bad as his marriage had gotten, to see her with another man, especially one as much of a scum bag as JoJo Sinclair, was more than he could bear. After listening to several minutes of JoJo trying to spin his way out while scrambling to put his clothes on, Percy had thrown the empty gun as hard as he could at JoJo, hitting him right under his left eye and sending blood everywhere. "Get the hell out of my house! And be thankful I didn't put a bullet in your head, you son of a bitch!!"

JoJo held a sock up to his face, trying to stop the bleeding as he ran to the door, one shoe on and one shoe still lying behind Percy's beautiful mahogany desk.

JoJo scanned the crowd at Harry's, hoping to see a client or two. When he spotted Percy he smiled and waved, turned to his date to tell her that he had to say hello to someone, then left her with the rest of his party and walked straight up to Percy and extended a hand. Percy noticed the beautiful cufflinks; the well-manicured cuticles, then looked up at JoJo and noticed the large ugly scar where Percy's Glock 19 hit him, and Percy finally smiled.

"So sorry to hear about the folks, Percy. I was out of town that entire week so I couldn't make it to the funeral. Just a terrible thing, I'm sure."

"Yes, it was pretty terrible JoJo, but believe it or not, I've been through worse."

"You're absolutely right there, Percy. Everything's relative, right?" JoJo was beginning to realize that it might have been a mistake to engage Percy in small talk as if nothing had ever happened. The strange smile on his face and the fiery eyes were beginning to worry JoJo. He glanced back at his party nervously.

"But you know what's NOT terrible, JoJo?" Percy was feeling it, the booze, and the moment. "What's NOT terrible is that fantastically awful freaking scar on your face. See, now every time you and I find ourselves together in public, I get the pleasure of looking at that ginormous disfiguring blob of tissue hanging off your ugly face right under your left eye, and it takes me back to happier times! Shall I tell your hot girlfriend over there how you got that grossly hideous scar, JoJo?"

"Look, Percy. I probably shouldn't have come over here. Just wanted to tell you that I was sorry to hear about Gilbert and Frances, that's all." JoJo scurried away as fast as he could. When he turned his back, Percy reached for his glass and was winding up to throw it when Billy grabbed his arm firmly and ripped the glass from his hand. "No throwing glasses at the customers, Percy. It's bad for business. You've had enough, buddy."

Thirty minutes later, Percy lay in his bed, the room spinning, hoping that tonight Beth wouldn't visit. He was in no condition to face her, not after allowing himself to revisit the 10 minutes that had destroyed his life.

◇ **11** ◇

A Thin Reed in a Gale

Melinda held Beth's hand and talked about forgiveness, about how it would be her first step to becoming whole again, about how she must view herself as someone worth forgiving. She opened her bible and read about Jesus kneeling down and writing something in the sand, and how a crowd full of self righteous men one by one had dropped the rocks they had picked up to stone an adulterous woman, of how Jesus had forgiven her and restored her self respect. This was all supposed to give her hope, and point her in a new direction, but it was making things so much worse until suddenly Beth turned on Melinda, and the words flew out loaded and hot.

"For you this is a story that may or may not have happened two thousand years ago, but my life isn't some story. I'm the woman caught in adultery, Melinda! It was me!! Percy walked in and saw me, caught me in the act in the house that he built for me, in his favorite room, in his favorite chair! He walked in on me having sex with a man he couldn't stand, there was no telling how long he had been standing there watching us! I betrayed the man who had given me everything I ever wanted. You should have seen the look on his face; I haven't been able to get it out of my mind for three years. It's the first thing I see in the morning and the last thought I have at night. So, thanks for the nice little story, but at 50 bucks an hour I was hoping for a little bit more than a bible study!"

She had slammed the door on her way out, driven home, collapsed on her bed and cried herself to sleep. During the night she had woken up, changed out of her clothes and walked downstairs for something to drink. She regretted blowing up at Melinda, the most tenderhearted, loving person she had ever met. She briefly thought of calling but noticed it was two o'clock in the morning. Instead, she opted for more self flagellation by going into the study.

Percy was waiting for her, sitting in his chair, staring at the stars through the Palladian window. She had noticed him before turning on the lights, so she had left them off, walked over to the rocker and sat down in the dark, holding on to her glass of milk with both hands. His visitations never startled her anymore. She had come to expect him, long for his appearances, for the chance to hear his voice and see his face.

"Of all the places in this great big old house, why here? Why did you choose to commit adultery right here in this chair?" He asked the question without emotion, without sarcasm, as if he was truly curious. Beth noticed the drink in his hand.

"Percy, please don't, not tonight, of all nights."

"What's so special about tonight?"

Beth leaned forward and placed her glass on the desk. Percy immediately chastised her for not using a coaster, fastidiously protective of his beloved desk even in her dreams. "For the past few weeks, I've been going to counseling. Today I had a rough session about this very topic. It's just not a good time."

"Yes, I suppose it's never really a good time to speak of betrayal."

"It's the single biggest regret of my life."

"Getting caught, you mean."

"No, I'm actually glad you walked in. I deserved to be caught. He had been coming on to me since my first day on the job... you know that. I had always put up with it and never really gave him a second thought in that way. But then you and I started falling apart, not that that's an excuse, there are no excuses, and that afternoon we had finished up a showing, I had to pick up something at the house and suddenly we were alone in here together. For some reason that I'll never understand, in that moment, I mean the moment right before anything had happened; I suddenly became so angry with you. I don't even remember what triggered it; I just remember suddenly being overwhelmed with anger and resentment. Then I looked at him, and just like that, I made the decision to do it. I suppose I wanted to punish you on some level, and maybe the reason we ended up in your chair was because of that. If it had been some random stranger, it wouldn't have cut you so badly, but JoJo? He was the perfect choice. So, it wasn't a weak moment. I wasn't taken advantage of. I just did a horrible, heartless, unspeakable thing that I knew would kill you. That's the sad truth."

Percy sat motionless in the chair, still staring out the window. "For someone who didn't want to talk about it, that's actually a pretty respectable answer."

There was a different sound to his voice in the darkness, Beth thought, deeper, more penetrating.

"You know I ran into him tonight... JoJo, over at Harry's..."

Even in the darkness, she could see that something was different. Percy was troubled, his hair misshapen, his clothes disheveled, everything about him wild and unkempt, lacking the ethereal grace that she had become accustomed to. For the first time she caught a whiff of vodka.

"There I was, minding my own business, when, of all people, JoJo walks in with his usual posse of sycophants, and just my luck he sees me at the bar. Next thing I know Billy is saving me from throwing something else at him. You know, he really needs a matching gash under the other eye; it would bring greater continuity to his face, don't you think?"

Reality is but a thin reed in a gale, and suddenly Beth had nothing to hold on to. Percy was a living, breathing thing, sitting across the desk from her. The realization raced through her bloodstream like a narcotic. The hairs on the back of her neck stood on end, a shiver ran down her back. She felt the beating of her heart in her temples, a feeling less of fear and more of thrill took control of her.

"So I couldn't sleep, couldn't even lie down." Percy leaned forward and rested his arms on the desk. "Then I remembered the key. You returned mine, so I thought it was about time I returned yours. You didn't answer the door, so I let myself in, poured myself a drink, and since this room played such a central role in tonight's festivities, I thought I would... return to the scene of the crime... as it were. I'm sorry. I had no right to come here."

"Don't leave." Beth could hardly breathe. Percy looked so defeated, so wounded. It was rare to see him this way, drinking and despondent. "I can't let you go; you've been drinking. Please stay. We can talk in the morning. Please don't go, not like this, not tonight."

They sat in silence for several long moments, both pondering the possibilities. Finally, Percy asked, "Was it your first time with him?"

"First and last... I swear to you." Another long silence and then Beth thought to add, "And there were never any others."

"Well, that's encouraging." Percy rose to his feet and had to steady himself. He hadn't been this drunk in years. "I'm ashamed to say that I am in no condition to drive."

Beth approached him cautiously. "You can sleep in the downstairs guest room if you like. Do you need any help getting in there?" Everything was electric between them, crackling with awkward tension. Beth was caught between rushing to his side and keeping a safe, discreet distance.

"Sure."

"Is that 'sure,' as in you want to sleep in the downstairs guest room, or 'sure,' as in you need some help walking in there?" Beth was rambling, caught up in the whirlwind.

"Both."

Beth slid her arm around his waist as he placed his arm around her shoulder, then they slowly walked out into the living room, then down a short hallway to the guest room. Percy's eyes were glassy and his eyelids heavy. She helped him into the bed, removed his shoes and thought to ask him for his car keys just in case. "Thanks for staying, Percy. I'll see you in the morning, Ok?"

Percy was already asleep. Beth turned out the light, walked upstairs and got into bed. She thought she might never get to sleep but was out in less than five minutes. At some point before dawn, seersucker Percy showed up at the foot of the bed, staring longingly at her, saying not a word. After several minutes, he walked over and got into the bed, wedging his body as close to hers as he could, holding her tight, just holding on to her silently. When the morning sun began to filter into the room through the crack in the drawn shades, Beth opened her eyes and he was gone. She glanced at the clock on the nightstand. Ten AM. She threw the covers off and scrambled to find her robe and go downstairs. She was furious at herself for sleeping so late. She needed to look after Percy, make him breakfast, make him want her again, make him never want to leave. Her heart raced as she ran down the stairs. The guest room door was opened. She ran to the front door and threw it open. Percy's car was gone. Back in the kitchen, there was a note on the counter. "I'm sorry. Had to leave. Thank you for not calling the sheriff. Percy."

Under the note was Percy's house key. "How did he leave? I had his keys," Beth thought. I took them from him and brought them upstairs and laid them on my nightstand.

The deep, mysterious waters of her dreams had never been murkier.

$$\diamond\ \textbf{12}\ \diamond$$

The Last Hope

Percy had been shocked by the judgment rendered in his divorce. He had assumed that since Beth had been caught in flagrante delicto, the proceedings would go his way. He hadn't spent very much time worrying about things until he discovered that Beth had hired a high powered divorce lawyer from Richmond. By the time he realized that his own lawyer was incompetent and intimidated, it was too late. Beth had gotten practically everything she had asked for, and Percy was left with half of his retirement account and $25,000 in cash.

The judgment had propelled him into despair. Instead of being embittered that Beth had gotten away with adultery, he had been overcome with regret for driving her away. What had been so awful about their first year together? They had won a fortune, had a blast doing it, and had put enough aside to pay cash for a McMansion. Half of America would have traded places with him, no questions asked. The thought had entered his mind late one night after some heavy drinking at Harry's. He would fix everything. He would take what money he had left and fly to Vegas. He would throw his silly scruples away, banish his misplaced guilt, and just be thankful for the gift. Not only would he win back all he lost in the settlement, but he might also win Beth back.

The next morning did not bring clarity. He jumped the first flight out, and by four o'clock in the afternoon, he was checked into his room and ready for some action. His first failure had been at roulette. One bet after another had failed. Percy was only partially alarmed; it had after all been over four years since he had been in a casino. Maybe it would take him a little time to get warmed up. But soon, it became obvious that something was very wrong. Every bet he made had been plagued by indecision and hesitation. He found himself thinking, thinking instead of just being, just reacting. It was a new sensation and a terrifying one. The 25 grand was gone by midnight.

Instead of limiting the damage, he had doubled down, drawing cash advances on every credit card in his wallet. Over the next three days he had racked up spectacular losses at blackjack, poker, even slots. He had hardly enough money left to pay his hotel bill and had arrived back home a broken mess. When he showed up on the front porch at 16 Jennings Lane, his mother had burst into tears at the sight of him, and Gilbert knew what had happened before any words were spoken. It was all ill-gotten gain. Nothing good ever comes from gambling money. He had warned him, but he hadn't listened, and now this red-haired Mata Hari had finally destroyed him, driving him to this nihilistic trip to Vegas. For the remaining four years of his life, Beth Hope's name would not be spoken in his house, and if she ever showed her face there, Gilbert had vowed to strangle her to death with his bare hands.

Gilbert and Frances had taken him in and tried to shelter him from the consequences of his own poor decisions. They set him up with councilors, then psychiatrists. No matter what they did, Percy sank deeper and deeper into depression. Then the awful night of his suicide attempt fell upon them with a knock on the door and the sweating face of the State Trooper.

"Your son may have attempted to take his own life; we pulled him out of the river not long ago. He is on the way to the hospital. I'll be glad to drive you there if you would like."

Frances had snuck out of his hospital room to call Beth. No matter how much she felt that most of this was Beth's fault, Frances thought it only fair that she heard the news from her. Maybe there still lived within Beth's soul an ounce of compassion, a shred of decency. But Beth never showed up. Percy lay there for two weeks and not a call or a visit. Frances finally had given up on Beth.

When he finally was discharged, they had managed to find Sheila Kennedy, and the long slow process of recovery had begun. Gilbert and Frances too had gone to counseling at Sheila's suggestion and had found it helpful. Their love for their son had been magnified under the blazing scrutiny of tragedy. Although they had been good parents, they hadn't been perfect, and identifying their shortcomings had helped them better understand their troubled son. Still, there were times of confusion and sadness. All of these new-fangled ways, all this blurring of distinctions between right and wrong, good and evil, all of these preening moral calculations, all of the elaborate justifications for what Gilbert and Frances understood to be moral failings and plain old sin were sometimes too much.

One night, as they sat on the front porch in silence after a long session, Gilbert had asked, "Why didn't they just settle down and have children? Why even get married at all? They were sleeping together before they got married, so why even bother with going through the ceremony if it wasn't because you wanted to start a family? Isn't that why we got married? I wanted to get on with life, have a child, and start something that would outlast me. They got married and just kept doing the same things, living the same way they had before. What was the point of it all? I guess maybe a child would have been an inconvenience. I don't suppose casinos have childcare. It's like it never occurred to either of them that life was about more than just the next fun thing, the next party, the next thrill. For the life of me, I just can't understand how anyone can live that way. We didn't teach him that, Frances. It was Beth."

Frances sat in silence. She had tossed around the same thoughts in her head a million times. No, they hadn't taught Percy to live for the moment, to think only of fun and thrill. But they had also not provided a very attractive alternative. They had plodded through their lives, following the laws to a fault, behaving themselves, taking no chances on anything that wasn't predictable. The coin of the realm had been dependability. They had lived a life of no surprises. Maybe Percy had wanted more, had wanted to be something other than merely reliable. She had broken the silence with, "Percy started gambling long before he ever laid eyes on Beth. Don't lay it all at her feet."

It had taken nearly two years for Percy to recover, and the time had taken a toll on all of them. Gilbert and Frances had rapidly aged as they watched their only child push himself back from the edge. It had only been a month or so after Percy had started to look and act like the son they knew when Frances had found Gilbert sprawled out awkwardly on the kitchen floor, unable to speak or move, a wild panic on his misshapen face. The stroke had begun the final chapter of their lives as a family. Just as Gilbert and Frances had tended to Percy's every need when he was born, so Percy would tend to them for the last 20 months of their existence. It was in this crucible of labor and tender care that Percy's life had been reclaimed. Trying to bring dignity and grace to his parents' dying days had restored his own dignity, giving him a keener appreciation for life itself and a better understanding of the value of devotion.

Yet, the dreaded day of their passing had been the first time it had ever dawned on Percy that he was the last Hope.

The dark fact that he was truly alone in the universe, with not another living soul who shared his blood had staggered him. The terrible thought, the crushing loneliness had hit him with full blunt force when he had looked up during the viewing and seen Beth signing the register. She was all he really had left. The woman who had nearly destroyed him was his only solid connection to life, and he hated her for it. Then the dreams had started forcing him to do battle with the hatred, a warfare of the heart played out late at night in his dreams, only with each passing skirmish Percy no longer could differentiate between real and unreal, substance and spirit. And now, he had crossed some sort of threshold by going to his old house, sitting in his old chair and sleeping downstairs from her beating heart. He no longer hated her, but worried about whether he could survive loving her again.

A Google Search

"Tell me about your parents." It was the second time Melinda had asked her the question, the first time during one of their sessions, and now at Panera's over soup and paninis, Beth's awkward attempt at an apology.

"You asked me that before."

"Yes, and you said you would rather not talk about them."

"Nothing has changed."

"Ok," Melinda looked at her with soulful eyes, full of regret and sadness. Beth wondered how one person could possibly care so much for another, knowing what Melinda knew about her. Melinda's earnestness, the apparently bottomless depths of her compassion were unsettling, even off-putting to Beth, who had never experienced such blind acceptance. To Beth, Melinda was equal parts saint and freak.

"There isn't anything to tell," Beth heard herself say. "I don't consider them parents at all in the first place, and secondly, I haven't heard from either of them since college, maybe 15 years ago."

"Why is that?"

"Why haven't I heard from them?" Beth stopped and leaned

back from the table. Was she seriously considering going down this road, telling this story to someone she had only known for a few months, but, if not Melinda, then who? "Ok, I never really had parents. What I had was a sperm donor and a womb."

Melinda listened to the story of a teenage party girl who got high and slept around a lot until the numbers caught up with her. For reasons Beth would never understand, this girl had decided to keep her baby. The father could have been one of many, but after some detective work and the process of elimination, he was identified as one Dillon Harrison. Luckily for this girl, he was from a relatively well-off family with strongly held religious beliefs. Although horrified at his behavior, an abortion was out of the question for the Harrisons, so the two of them were wed in a Justice of the Peace ceremony attended by virtually no one. She had moved into the Harrison home since her own parents wanted nothing to do with her.

The baby was born and within a couple of years, strongly held religious beliefs notwithstanding, the marriage was over, and the girl refused to give the child to the Harrisons to raise, which obviously would have been the right thing to do. The girl had grown to despise them for treating her like a cancerous tumor that had attached itself to their idyllic family for two years. So, she took the baby and carved out an existence for the two of them as beneficiaries of the modern welfare state. But, the monetary restraints of the system didn't allow enough spending money to facilitate her old carefree party life, so this ever-resourceful single mother did what single mothers had done for millennia. She was a natural for the oldest profession, young, beautiful and fearless. But over time her new lifestyle sucked the youth and beauty out of her, and life began to resemble something like hell. Every now and then, Dillon would visit to see how she was doing, but the visits ended after a while. When the child was 13, the ever-vigilant State had intervened and placed her in a home for girls, from which the possibility of an emancipating adoption was five percent. The best the child could do was a couple of foster homes with indifferent care, but from the stories she had heard, she had been thankful for mere indifference.

Somewhere along the line she had taken intelligence tests in school and been identified as "gifted," a title that had filled her with silent anger, since she could find not one thing about her existence that looked like a gift. When she graduated from high school, she had been given a scholarship to attend the University of Maryland, one of the rare affirmative action stipends set aside for poor white trash, that shuffled her from social services over to the State University with the fervent hope that at some point in the not too distant future, Beth Harrison might one day drop off of the public teat. It was the second greatest break of her life, going to college. It had gone well; she had made friends and learned of the possibilities of life. She had discovered that she was smart, capable, and most of all, beautiful. At long last she had managed an escape from hell.

Beth was exhausted. She had never shared her story with anyone. She looked into Melinda's eyes to see if there was any love left. Melinda was crying.

"So, you haven't heard from either one of them in over 15 years? Have you tried to contact them?"

"No. Why would I want to make contact with them? They've had 15 years to contact me. My father probably hasn't given me a second thought for 30 years, and I would be shocked if my mother was still alive. They don't matter anymore. What's done is done."

They sat in silence. Beth thought it odd that Melinda was the one crying, while she had felt nothing, not even relief from the unburdening. She just sat there feeling cold and empty.

"What was her name?... your mother?"

"Jill." Beth hadn't spoken the name in years. "Her name was Jill."

Melinda had stopped crying and that effortless smile had

returned to her face. "Well, I can think of one thing that Jill did right. She made the decision to give you life, and I'm very grateful she did." She reached out and grabbed Beth's hand.

The words had stunned her, caught her off guard. Finally, the tears came. The crushing, suffocating truth was that Beth Hope had walked 35 years on the earth, and there was only one other human being alive who was glad that she was born, and that person was sitting across the table from her, three months ago, a total stranger.

"By the way, you said earlier that getting that scholarship to college was the second best break you've ever received in your life. What was the best?"

"Being asked to be a bridesmaid at Katherine Miller's wedding."

* * *

Percy had taken a long shower, letting the hot water pour over his pounding head. He only got out when the hot water stopped coming. He got dressed, tried to eat something and took more Advil for his well-earned headache. Percy felt alternating waves of embarrassment and excitement when he pondered his actions of the past 24 hours. Throwing a shot glass at JoJo would have been an unmitigated disaster; thank God for Billy. Trespassing in Beth's house, drunk, had been a juvenile prank born of emotional desperation. Beth's tender response had warmed his soul like no single thing he could remember from his life. She hadn't thrown him out, hadn't cut him with sharp accusations, had, in fact, been honest with him in a tone of voice unidentifiable from the many he had heard before. Slipping into bed with her had been like a dream, feeling the warmth of her skin, the comforting, familiar scent of her hair. Ever since the passing, Percy had felt adrift, unmoored from anything substantial. But from the moment that he had held her, he felt a connection to the world, like he was finally attached to something real. Then it had hit him just how foolish and dangerous a thing it was to be in his ex-wife's bed uninvited. Suddenly, reality had intruded on his beautiful dream, and reality had scared him to death. He had grabbed his keys from the nightstand, left a note on the kitchen counter and crawled home.

Now, he sat in his meager library sorting through a week's worth of mail that lay unopened on his desk, contemplating his reckless foolishness, and wondering what he would say to her if she called. Sam sat at his feet on the floor, his head tilted to one side, one ear flopped open, eyes moist and tender staring holes into Percy.

* * *

Melinda asked another question, this one from a place of confusion, "Beth, you said that this is the first time you've ever told anyone about your parents. You mean besides Percy, right?"

"No... Percy doesn't know."

"Wait, you married him but never told him about your parents? He never asked? I don't understand."

"I told him that they both died when I was a kid. Actually, I told him lots of things about my life that weren't true. Look Melinda, Percy fell for me because I was the hottest thing he had ever seen in his life. I wasn't about to break that spell with this story. Good looks can only get a girl so far. He was my meal ticket to a better life. Besides, he was so smitten with me he didn't much care about what had preceded him. We just rode the wave of passion right to the church and never looked back. I know that sounds awfully shallow and manipulative, but it's the truth. He didn't want to know, and I didn't want to tell him. Case closed."

Melinda looked pale with astonishment. "But how in the world can he possibly understand you without knowing you, knowing all of you? Beth, you say that you love him and you want forgiveness, that you want another chance with him. Don't you think that a good place to start would be... honesty?"

"I don't know how to answer you. I should say yes, I know. But honesty hasn't been everything you make it out to be for me. This world runs on lies, it's the fuel of life. I can't just abandon it for pure honesty all of a sudden. Baby steps, Melinda, baby steps."

* * *

The monitor provided the only light in the room. It was some time after midnight. Beth sat mesmerized by the information that had materialized instantly on her computer screen, three pages of it all from a simple Google search for "Dillon Harrison." No pictures, but they wouldn't have done her any good since she had not even a foggy recollection of him. There were some spellings, such as "Dylan," which couldn't be right. She did remember the spelling, oddly enough. Most of the entries were for Facebook pages, and since she didn't have one, they weren't of much help either. How could there be so many of them? Beth had always felt the name Dillon was so unique, even exotic, but it was a big country and there lived 19 correctly spelled Dillon Harrisons in the United States of America, from Maine to Arizona. At least he wasn't Bob or Mike.

Beth shut the computer off and sat in the darkness. What was she doing? If one of the 19 were her father, what possible difference would it make? He will have forgotten her, or worse, turn out to be some child molesting asshole. Nothing good could come from tracking him down, nothing. And yet, here she was at two o'clock in the morning wondering what he looked like, trying to imagine meeting him, shaking his hand, hearing his voice. It was insanity, a sudden and swift obsession brought on by her snap decision to tell the truth about her life to Melinda, the porcelain angel of a preacher's wife with the southern accent, whose eyes could melt a heart of stone. But, "Christ-centered counseling" was too heavily wrapped up in brutal honesty for its own good. People who went around telling everyone the truth all the time could get into serious trouble. All of this baring your soul fearlessly before a loving God sounded fine in the abstract, but the very idea of calling Percy up to inform him that he did have ex-in-laws after all, only she had no idea where they lived because she hadn't spoken to them in 15 years, seemed like a terrible conversation starter and the absolute end of any hopes she had for reconciliation. But ever since the night that Percy had held her close in bed, Beth had wanted nothing more in the world than one more chance with him. Lies hadn't worked, maybe the truth would. So, she called him early the next morning and asked if they could meet somewhere, that there was something she needed to tell him, and it was the sort of thing that must be discussed face to face. The telephone wouldn't do. Harry's for lunch was suggested; too loud and not private enough. Then Percy had said, "Well, why don't you just come over here?"

Sam barked as soon as Beth's Mercedes pulled into the driveway, then greeted Beth with wild enthusiasm. As usual, Beth ignored him the best she could. She was not a dog person. They sat across from each other at the kitchen table; the tacky Formica-topped one with the curved aluminum legs. Beth had thought it hideous when she had first seen it and, no doubt, had said so. And here it was 12 years later, outlasting Gilbert, Frances, and her marriage. Damned stuff was indestructible.

"You look great." Percy smiled at Beth for maybe the first time in a decade.

"Please don't do this, Percy," she thought. "Don't go all nice and considerate on me now, not with what I'm about to tell you."

"You know, I've picked up the phone a hundred times to call you since the other night, and I just didn't have the guts to dial the number. I was so out of line. But I wanted to apologize for walking out like I did. You had been so kind to me, and you had every right to throw me out..."

"Please, no! Percy, don't do this. You've got to give me a chance to talk."

"Listen, Beth, I know we have a truly horrible history, but..."

"Percy, Stop!" Beth had reached out and touched his hands, then pulled them quickly away in embarrassment. "Don't say anything else until you hear what I have to say. If I don't get this out now, I might never have the strength to do it again."

Percy sat back and listened to the tortured wreck of a story that was Beth's life before she had met him. He said nothing, just listened and never took his eyes off hers. It was a skill that she had taught him. He who looks away first loses is the way Beth had framed it back in the day. But Percy wasn't concerned with winning or losing now. He had nothing else to lose anyway. It was the second time in two days that she had told it, and this time the tears came, silently, but relentlessly down her face. She left out nothing, bared it all, even her recent discovery of the 19 Dillons. Percy had gotten up once to get her a tissue, and then sat back down, pushing himself further away from the table while crossing his arms across his chest, a bad sign Beth had thought. She had finished with the words, "I have no idea what I would say to him if I ever did find him. I'm not even sure it's not the worst idea I've ever come up with, but something in my heart tells me I should pursue him."

Sam had laid on the half circle rug in front of the refrigerator for the duration of their conversation, but now that they had stopped talking, he rose up slowly and walked over beside Beth and placed his head in her lap. She patted his head gently as she cried.

The silence at 16 Jennings Lane was complete and intolerable until Percy broke it with, "If I thought I had a blood relative alive somewhere in this world, let alone a father, I would move heaven and earth to find them, and it wouldn't matter to me whether they had a rap sheet a mile long." Once again, he smiled. Then it was his turn to hold her hand across the table. "Listen to me, Beth. You need to hire a private investigator. I have one you can use. If your dad is alive, my guy will find him. Then you need to go see him. You'll never be able to move forward unless you do this. It might be a terrible meeting, but it might also change your life."

"I just don't think I have the courage to go through with this."

"I'll go with you. Maybe if we combine forces there will be one less coward to deal with."

"That doesn't make any sense."

"No, it doesn't. Sounded good in my head though."

"I can't ask you to do this."

"You didn't ask. I offered."

"What will you do with Sam? I don't think I could make it to Maine and back, sharing a truck with a dog."

"My neighbors will watch him for me. Ted and Bea love him as much as I do."

Two weeks later the PI's report identified Beth's father as a lawyer, aged 51, divorced, with two grown children, living in Camden, Maine. Over the Thanksgiving holiday, Beth and Percy would make the drive up in Percy's gas-guzzling pickup truck, with no idea what they would find, or how they would be received, or even if they would be received. Everything about the trip had disaster written all over it, not the least of which was the fact that Beth couldn't even get in Gilbert's beast of a truck without assistance. But at least neither one of them would be alone, feeling forsaken on Thanksgiving.

◇ **14** ◇

Road Trip

Percy picked her up on the Wednesday morning before Thanksgiving. If either of them had been thinking clearly, they would have picked practically any other day of the year to begin an 800-mile drive up I-95. The most costly, nerve-wracking and dangerous drive in America would have been terrible any day of the year, but on Thanksgiving Eve it was simply foolish. But, neither of them wanted to be alone on their favorite holiday, so there was Percy, hoisting all of Beth's luggage into the covered bed of the Dodge, then showing her the proper form needed to climb into the leather bucket seat.

"Good God-Almighty! I'll need a step ladder to get into this thing. I don't want to even think about how I'm supposed to get down from up here." Percy thought he saw a brief smile right before he shut her door and walked around to climb up himself. All night long he tossed and turned, wondering how weird it was going to be to be in a vehicle with her for the first time in years, for hours and hours. What would they talk about? Was this one of his dumbest ideas of all time? The very idea of Beth in a pickup truck seemed ridiculous to him, but now it was too late, there would be no turning back.

They backed out of the driveway and made their way to the entry ramp onto 95 without a word. With every mile, the pressure became more intense for someone to say something. Finally Percy offered, "Would you like to listen to some music?"

Beth stared out at the countryside racing by. Percy could see her breath fogging up the window. She made no reply at first, then said to no one in particular, "Man, how weird is this?"

The words had sounded more like a sigh than a question. Percy couldn't think of a reply, but then settled on, "Yes, I suppose it is a bit weird. You and I haven't been in a car together for years, and suddenly we find ourselves in a truck on a road trip to Maine."

"Why am I doing this? Why are you doing this? Better yet, why are WE doing this?" Beth seemed like any minute she was going to call the whole thing off. Percy could see tears forming in her eyes. Suddenly, he blurted out, "We're doing this because it's the right thing to do. Now, we've got a long drive ahead of us. You're going to need to take it easy. Just relax."

Beth turned towards him. "Well, at the very least we need some ground rules on what we can and can't talk about, or we're going to end up arguing about the past and killing each other."

"Fair enough. Let's not talk about the past." Percy wanted to be agreeable.

"But the past is all we have." Beth seemed nervous and unsure of her ground. "How about we make a rule that all conversations must start with a question?"

"Like, why are you such a jerk?"

"Exactly."

"Well, I already asked you a question and you ignored me."

"What question?"

"I asked you if you wanted to listen to any music."

"You did? Oh yeah... sure."

They drove through Fredericksburg in awkward, pressurized silence. By the time they had reached Occoquan the traffic had slowed to a crawl. Beth sat up straight and blurted out, "How come you had a private investigator's name so handy the other night? Have you ever had me followed?"

"Actually, that's two questions."

"Well, did you?"

"Yes." Percy felt not the slightest hesitation in telling her the truth. Anyone in his position would have done the same thing. She had cheated on him, and he needed to know if she was a serial adulteress. Beth slumped back into her seat and turned her gaze towards the endless kingdom of asphalt that was Northern Virginia. "... and, what did your investigator discover?"

"That with the exception of the one unfortunate mistake, you were a paragon of virtue."

"I wouldn't go that far." It would be her last words until Baltimore.

She reached into her bag and took out the yellow folder with the black and white photographs of Dillon Harrison. There was only one close-up. The resemblance was uncanny; they had the same smile, same teeth, and same expressive eyes. He was handsome. He dressed well, in that calculated, meticulous style of the wealthy, well-tailored sports jackets, starched cotton shirts, neatly pressed dress khakis with the razor-edged crease down the front. When she thought of meeting him she became sick to her stomach, so she hustled the pictures back in the folder and put everything away.

"I could use a cigarette."

"You smoke?"

"No, but I've been thinking about starting."

"'I could use a cigarette' was not in the form of a question."

"What, are you Alex Trebek now?"

"Uh, these were your rules; I'm just trying to maintain order here."

"Ok, ok. You wouldn't happen to have a cigarette, would you?"

"No! What do I look like, an idiot? Besides, even if I did, I couldn't possibly let you smoke it in this awesome truck."

They went back and forth for a while about the truck, making fun of each other like in the old days. The mood would lift for miles at a time until Beth would leave him chasing some dark thought. She would fall silent and stare out the window again, focusing on nothing, suffering from some indefinable loss. Percy watched her and wondered what had become of her mother, whether Dillon Harrison might know, then worrying that the news might be bad. Shortly after crossing into New Jersey, they stopped for gas and lunch at one of those dreadfully filthy State-run rest areas. They filled up the 20-gallon tank, calculating that they were getting 15 miles per gallon, then stood in line at Burger King for 20 minutes to get their made ten hours ago and recently taken out of the microwave, Whoppers. The tables were so grimy they ate in the car instead. Percy cranked up the sound system and chose Beethoven's Ninth Symphony. After a few minutes, Beth interrupted.

"I'm sorry. I've got nothing against classical music. Some of it's actually nice. But, we're in the parking lot of a Burger King in freaking New Jersey. That music might get us killed." She sat aside her fries, reached into her bag and pulled out a CD. "Here, try this instead."

Percy saw the words, "Country Party Mix" written in permanent marker across the front. Soon, everyone from Merle Haggard and Willie Nelson to Brad Paisley and Carrie Underwood were belting out ballads about cheating, good women gone bad, the dangers of a woman scorned, the wonder of trucks, dogs and cold beer. Percy couldn't help noticing the irony.

The hours in New Jersey seemed interminable, first the New Jersey turnpike, then the Garden State Parkway with its toll booths dragging traffic to a crawl every 15 minutes. It was getting colder outside, and by the time they reached the New York State line, the sun was lower in the sky, sending long shadows across the interstate. After the country music had cycled through a few times, Beth asked for something more peaceful. Percy suggested Debussy, and within 20 minutes she was asleep.

Percy glanced at her as she lay still, head against the window. She was still a beautiful woman, her face still nearly perfect. He marveled at how little she had aged through all of the torment of recent years. Watching her made Percy sad, not because of what he had lost, but what she was about to lose. Percy couldn't imagine the meeting going well. If Harrison was as well off as advertised, certainly he would have had the means to reach out to Beth long before now. Percy could only conclude that, for whatever reason, he wanted nothing to do with a mistake from his intemperate youth. But even if there was the slightest chance of a reasonably happy ending, it was a chance worth taking, or at least he had thought so before seeing Beth, beautiful, beguiling Beth, asleep in the passenger seat of his truck. Now, all he cared about was protecting her, shielding her from a cold rejection.

Soon, it was dark. They had been on the road for close to nine hours and Percy's legs were beginning to cramp. They were somewhere northeast of Hartford, close to the Massachusetts State line, when he saw the Hampton Inn sign.

Percy paid for a suite. Beth said nothing as they checked in, and after they unloaded their luggage, she had offered no opinion on where they should go for dinner. It fell to Percy to take the lead. He drove them a couple of miles down the road until he came to one of those ghastly places near major interstate exchanges where all you can see for miles is one national chain restaurant after another, all piled up on top of each other. The air was thick with the competitive fragrances of America. Olive Garden's pasta alfredo was battling with the USDA Grade A prime rib of Longhorns, while the distinct aroma of ground horse meat slathered with taco sauce poured forth from the take-out window of Taco Bell. Finally they had stumbled upon what looked like a local barbeque joint with a parking lot packed with cars on a Wednesday night. Percy had found a spot and was preparing to get out of the truck when Beth grabbed his arm.

"Percy, I'm really sorry, but I just don't feel like going in. Can you maybe ask if we can get something to go? I'm really sorry. I should have said something before now, I know."

"Well, sure. They probably have take-out. You want me to order for both of us?"

"Would you please?"

When Percy returned to the truck a half an hour later with two containers of beef brisket, two orders of turnip greens and a bag of hush puppies, he half expected Beth to be gone. But, there she was, looking gorgeous, and thankful. Back at the hotel, Percy had found plates, knives, forks and napkins in the kitchen, and had used two dish towels for placemats on the coffee table. They were both starving, and the barbeque was respectable considering that it had been made by a Connecticut Yankee. Percy finished first, like always, then sat back and watched Beth.

"So, when did you lose your gift?" Percy asked, trying to start a conversation the correct way.

"Which one? I have so many."

"You know which one I'm talking about, your mind reading talent."

"Who says I have?"

"I can just tell."

"You can, huh? I can tell you what you're thinking right now." Beth picked up the last hush puppy, took a bite of it, and smiled. "You're looking at me right now wondering what I look like naked, wondering if I've lost anything."

Percy laughed out loud. "That doesn't prove a thing; you could say that about any man on the face of the earth who had spent nine hours in a truck with you, and you'd be right!"

"That's very sweet of you to say, Percy. The truth is, I can't read you anymore. I guess it's because I don't know you like I used to."

The air had become suddenly thick with tension. Beth got up from her chair and walked around the coffee table, sat down next to Percy on the sofa, and held his hand. Her touch was softer than he had remembered, the smell of her hair intoxicating, but she was trembling. "Percy, I don't even know if tracking my father down is the right thing to do. To tell the truth, the closer we get to Maine the worse I feel. But, I do know that being with you, having you with me, means more to me than you'll ever know." She looked into his eyes and moved closer to kiss him when Percy placed his fingertips on her lips.

"Beth, as much as I would love to kiss you, I think we both need to slow down. Over the next few days, both of us are going to have to do some very clear thinking. I don't think we should add you and me to the mix. Let's keep our heads clear until we meet your father, then we can see where we stand. That big old King sized bed in the other room is yours. I'll sleep out here on the pullout. I think that's best, don't you?"

Beth threw her arms around his neck. She knew he was right. She was grateful that at least one of them was an adult. After a good night kiss on the cheek, she looked back at him at the door to her room, "Why in God's name did I ever leave someone like you?"

❖ **15** ❖

Dillon Harrison

The next day, after several hours of driving, they finally arrived at the Piscataqua River Bridge with its green steel arches leading them into Maine. They soon left the interstate highway system in favor of the coastal road that snaked its way through small harbor towns from Kittery all the way to New Brunswick. Although they had a horrible time, the scenery was beautiful, and getting away from four lanes of bumper-to-bumper traffic brought with it a measure of peace and serenity that Percy thought was greatly needed at this point in their journey. Beth's spirits seemed to lift as they drove through each town. It was a clear day with a bright autumn sun lighting up the ocean. By lunchtime they found themselves in the Perkins Cove section of the town of Ogunquit. They got out of the truck and quickly realized how cold it was, the bright sun had deceived them. They found an adorable little place to eat. There was a covered deck overlooking the ocean with old, rusted propane heaters every few feet to take the chill away. Beth looked calm and peaceful, as if she hadn't a care in the world.

"You know, if we were still married, this would be one hell

94

of a vacation. If you don't end up killing me by the end of this trip, we should remember this place." Beth was trying to be casual, trying to forestall any talk of her father, any reminder of the business at hand, business that was now less than 120 miles away.

"Have you ever been up here? This is my first trip this far north."

"Me too. I've been to New York City a bunch of times and once I spent a weekend in Boston, but that's about it." Beth ordered another beer from the waiter; a college aged kid with the worst accent she had ever heard. She had heard about the unique Maine accent but had never experienced it in the flesh. It was all she could do to keep from laughing out loud. But, she wondered if he was just as amused with the thick, slower drawl of her Virginia accent. She poured the beer in her glass straight up and watched the head spill over the edge at the end, just like Gilbert always did.

"Do you think it's strange that neither of his kids will be with him for Thanksgiving? What was it your guy said? They were both out of the country on a cruise with their mother? I think that's strange that they wouldn't be together, don't you?"

Percy looked at Beth and noticed that she hadn't taken her eyes off the ocean in quite a while, hadn't made eye contact with anyone, even the waiter, since they had sat down for lunch. On a dime she had shifted from strange calmness to nervous agitation.

"It is a little odd, but the kids live with their mother, and they have been divorced for six years now, so maybe it's not too terribly strange."

"You know I'm terrified, right?" Beth finally looked up at him, and she looked for a moment like a little child.

"Yes. Of course you are. I'm scared myself and we're not even..." Percy caught himself.

"Married anymore?" Beth finished the sentence for him.

"Well, you know what I mean. I guess what I'm trying to say is that since the passing, I'm alone in the world, for the first time, truly alone. And until a few days ago I thought you were too. But now, we discover that you have a father, a half-sister and a half-brother and maybe a mother alive somewhere too. Do you have any idea what I would give for that, to know that there was someone else who shared my blood, my ancestry?"

"You're not alone, Percy. You have me."

"Yes. Yes, Beth, you're right. I have you, an ex-wife who forced me into bankruptcy, and a suicide attempt."

"I thought we agreed not to talk about the past?"

Percy had regretted the words as soon as he had heard them fly out of his mouth, so blunt, and callous. This was not the time or place. "You're right. We both agreed. I'm sorry, that was a mean and hateful thing to say. Forget I ever said it. Let's just rewind the tape, Ok?"

"No, no. It's out there now. You can't unring that bell. It's been established that I'm a terrible human being, and I accept your judgment. But, am I beyond redemption? Do you think it's possible for me to change, for anyone to change? Isn't that what this trip is about? Didn't we attempt this reconnection with my father because we believe there's a chance of making something good and healthy out of something bad and painful?

"Of course I do. You already have changed Beth."

"Good. But, just so you know, life with you wasn't always moonlight and magnolias for me either."

"And I accept your judgment."

Every new town brought fresh delights of sights, sounds, and smells, the air pungent with brininess, the toll of ships' bells skimming over the placid water of picturesque bays stocked full of sail boats large and small.

Percy found himself wishing the drive would never end. As the sun began to lower on the horizon, the harbor would turn first a soft yellow and then blaze out in fiery orange just before the sun disappeared from view. Camden was brightest of all, as they had arrived at the peak of a brilliant November sunset. Percy found the Lord Camden Inn on Main Street, just down the street from the office of Dillon Harrison, Esquire.

As soon as they had walked into the lobby, Percy knew that he had made the wrong choice. As pedestrian as the Hampton Inn had been, the Lord Camden Inn looked like the sort of place that trust fund couples came to celebrate their tenth wedding anniversaries. Everyone in the place had that well-tanned, perfectly groomed look, the kind of people you would find on the pages of high gloss "Living Well" magazines. It wasn't that he couldn't afford this sort of place, but it wasn't appropriate for the mission. He thought that they should be at a seedier type of place where there's a pulsing red neon sign hanging on the building outside the window keeping you up all night. There should be an occasional gunshot down on the street. Percy should have to go over and pull down a cracked and faded yellow shade and check the street to make sure they hadn't been followed. Instead, their view was the majestic masts of 70-foot polished wooden sailboats bobbing up and down slowly in Camden harbor off in the distance, and the brightly painted and shuttered boutiques that lined Main Street below. Their room would have made a perfect Honeymoon suite with the tray of chocolate-dipped strawberries on the table for two over next to the balcony, if it hadn't been for the two queen beds. Percy was embarrassed and thought he should offer some sort of explanation when Beth turned to him and said, "You are the man! This place is like a dream."

"I didn't realize it was so... nice. Probably should have booked that Super 8 we passed back outside of Rockport. This place feels wrong."

"It feels perfect to me. If I'm about to be disappointed, I may as well sleep in comfort. I'm hungry. Where can we eat?

Will anything be open on Thanksgiving night?"

"Let's go find out."

Percy and Beth asked the concierge in the lobby, and he advised, "Cappy's is always open. They have the best clam chowder in town. Nothing fancy, really just a bar with pub grub, but it's gonna be your best bet tonight."

Cappy's was just a block from the hotel, fronting Main Street and backing up to the bay. It was a cramped but charming two story bar with extremely low ceilings, which gave it the feel of something ghost-ridden and ancient. There were just a handful of people in the place, so the upstairs was off limits, making nervous tourists wonder what might go on upstairs at Cappy's. The lone waitress showed them to a table in the back that offered a view of the twinkling lights of the harbor. The entire building smelled like the sea. The clam chowder was glorious even though it came served in a shiny tin cup with a smiling lobster laminated on the side. Percy had ordered two lobster rolls since he had read somewhere that you should never leave Maine without eating a lobster roll. As far as he could tell, the ingredients consisted of fresh lobster meat, and lots of it, mixed with a couple of tablespoons of mayonnaise and stuffed to overflowing on a fried-in-butter sub roll. It was like eating a heaven sandwich. When the second beers arrived, Percy heard the ringing of the tiny bell that was attached to the front door. He glanced up and saw Beth's father enter and take a seat at the bar.

◇ **16** ◇

A Series of Fixes

Dillon Harrison unlocked the door to his Main Street law office at four o'clock in the afternoon on Thanksgiving Day, in a horrible mood. He had spent the morning brooding around his house on Lake Megunticook, resentful of being alone and abandoned by his children. It was one thing for them to be away with their mother, another entirely to not even bother to call. But he had become accustomed to this sort of treatment. In the years since the divorce, he had lost the battle for hearts and minds, lost the fight for public opinion, and although his kids still loved him, their loyalties were with their mother, and why not? His had been a self-inflicted wound, a series of weak and reckless moments. It had been this way his entire life. Dillon Harrison just couldn't keep it in his pants, and it had finally cost him his family.

So, today he would make another installment payment on the unredeemable debt of his transgressions. He would refuse all invitations from friends to eat Thanksgiving dinner with them; he would inflict the maximum pain possible by going it alone, sitting on the deck overlooking the still water of the lake and flipping through picture albums from happier times,

99

such was the sadistic nature of his penance. The football game would be on in the background as he ate his ham sandwich and chips. He would take a short, unsatisfying nap. Then he would make the five-minute drive into Camden and its virtually abandoned streets to sit in his office for a while. The well of his guilt was deep.

His law practice was thriving, he being a big legal fish in this very small backwater pond; he was well respected in town, he was healthy, still had his looks, but as he sat down at his desk and started shuffling through the papers in front of him, an overwhelming feeling of failure washed over him. His life had been a series of bad decisions, of personal failings that no amount of professional success, no powers of intellect or reason could mollify. In his heart Dillon Harrison knew that he was a man of expedience, a self-interested climber whose life had been cobbled together by a series of fixes, none greater than the very first fix.

Dillon had grown up in a home built upon the unshakable foundation of God's Word. For Charles and Joy Harrison there existed no contingency in life for which the Word of God didn't prescribe a remedy. If one simply followed God's "Owner's Manual," one would prosper. If calamity or scandal was unleashed upon a family, it was because of willful sin and rebellion against sacred scripture. All was well until the day shortly after Dillon's 16th birthday when it was revealed that he had impregnated the most notorious party girl at Lewiston High School. Charles and Joy Harrison's oldest son, starting shortstop on the baseball team, starting point guard on the basketball team, and President of his sophomore class, had engaged in drunken, pre-marital sex with a full-figured, red-haired trollop from the wrong side of the tracks. What made matters so much worse was the equally dreaded news that she had no intention of having an abortion. It had been the day when theory met reality for the Harrisons. It was as if their entire belief system had been side-swiped by a hit-and-run pickup truck with a Planned Parenthood bumper sticker. Their fundamental belief in the sanctity of life took on sinister dimensions when the life in question lived within such a reprehensible slut.

After much prayer, soul searching, and fasting, the Harrisons had come to the decision to trust God and follow the dictates of their consciences and Holy Scripture. Dillon would marry Jill Chester, at age 16, the barely legal minimum age in Maryland. She would live in their home. She would give birth to the child, and Dillon's parents would immediately begin plotting an exit strategy that would rid them all of mother and child before Dillon went off to college to begin his life. They could endure the whispers in the community, the sneers from their church friends at Melrose Methodist Church, who all along had thought that the Harrisons were too good to be true, and had been secretly thrilled at their humiliation. They could put up with all of it if, in the end, it didn't ruin Dillon's life.

His mother's strategy of showering Jill with a thousand small cruelties had paid handsome dividends, embittering her to the point that she agreed to a divorce, and insisted on full custody of the child. Dillon had always been The Prince to his mother's Machiavelli, but watching her machinations over the two years he and Jill were together taught him lessons he would carry with him forever. One must do whatever works, whatever is expedient, without regret or remorse, a bloodless pragmatism, it's how people got along in the world. Disentangled from Jill, Dillon was free to pursue the life of success and achievement he was meant to enjoy, and he did so with vigor and abandon. But throughout that pursuit he dragged around with him, Marley-like, a weight of loss and regret. No matter how hard he tried, he couldn't leave behind the memory of his child. It had been his silent companion, the obsession of every spare thought. What was she like? What would become of her? It would become his recurring dream, a constant reminder of failure.

So, he would spend the afternoon in his office, his trophy room. It was here where he could believe that he was a good man. He loved the law, loved protecting his clients from its misapplication, and loved winning. In his meticulously decorated office, the finer points of his victories were on display, along with his perfect family in photographs that lined the credenza behind his desk. He had never removed those containing his ex-wife. She was his wife once, and would always be their mother. Removing all evidence of her seemed inappropriately petty. So, there she was, flowing blonde hair, nine years younger, flanked by the twins on the day of their graduation from high school. There she was again with them at Disney World when they were just in grade school, faces alive with excitement. They had taken so many perfect pictures over the years.

But there were no pictures of Elizabeth, no pictures of his first born. For those, he would have to open the safe under the cabinet in the conference room. He would pull out the fireproof Army green metal box, set it on his desk and fish the key out of its hiding place. Inside would be his collection of newspaper clippings and photographs documenting the life of Elizabeth Harrison. Most of them dated from her time at the University of Maryland. She was so beautiful, had overcome so much, gone so far in the world without the advantages he had been born with, without a father. There was her bridal picture from the Times-Dispatch, a picture of her with her new husband, the graduate student. He had only made one trip to Virginia. The construction permit for her new house had been published in the business section. He had the address and had gone to see it. He had kept a safe distance away and took a picture from inside his rental car. He had had dinner at Harry's and watched them together. They looked happy, even joyous. It was all he had ever wanted for her, and all he had needed to see. It would be his one and only trip to Virginia.

Then he had gotten the news of the divorce, and the salacious details of Percy's collapse. It did no good to mourn for her. Getting caught committing adultery only meant that she was a chip off the old block. Dillon took personal responsibility for the failure of his estranged daughter's marriage. It was only fair. The poor girl had been the product of a womanizer and a hard-partying slut. What chance did she have?

He put away the pictures, returned the box to the safe and noticed the brilliant orange sky outside, another November sunset on the coast of Maine. He paid a few bills, organized his calendar for the following week and then felt in desperate need of a drink. He would walk to Cappy's. There would be hardly anyone in the place, so he wouldn't have to make small talk or parcel out free legal advice. He could just take the edge off in peace. He had taken his jacket off, draped it over the back of his bar stool and ordered a drink. As he began to scan the room, he saw them both at the table in the back, staring at him. It was them, had to be. He would recognize that red hair anywhere. He quickly looked away and turned to face the street. His heart was beating like a thousand drums and his hands began to shake. "Oh, my God..."

As the blood raced through his veins, the lawyer who lived in his brain came to his rescue. Dillon began to regain his composure. It was like 11th-hour evidence or a client self-destructing on the witness stand; although disconcerting, it could be overcome with detached calm and the power of reason over panic. This was probably a chance encounter born of the vagaries of fate. If not, then his 34-year-old daughter and her ex-husband had tracked him down for one of several reasons. They had either come here to confront him for his manifold failings as a father and human being, or out of curiosity, or because they hoped to extract from him some form of compensation for 30 years of pain and suffering. If the latter, there wasn't enough money in the world, and even if there were, the law was on his side. Of these three, he desperately wished to be confronted with his sins. He wanted to agree with every accusation and even add a few of his own, then release her forever from the tedious curse of ever having to give him another thought.

He gave another peek over his shoulder. She was gone, and Percy was headed towards the front door. He would pass by only a few feet from the back of his bar stool. Dillon leaned in closer to the bar and took a long drink.

"Excuse me, but are you Dillon Harrison?"

The accent was unmistakable... *eckuuze me, but arr you Dillun Herrrisun?* It had to be him, Percy Hope. Dillon turned around slowly and managed a smile. "Yes, I am. Can I help you?" Elizabeth was either in the ladies' room or had left by the back door.

"Well, I certainly hope so. My wife and I are from out of town, and we recently bought a cabin out on the Lake for a summer place and we will be closing at the end of the month. Several people have given us your name because we will be needing a closing attorney, and well, we were wondering if we could come to see you tomorrow about the details?" As Percy heard himself say the words, it sounded so fake, ill-conceived, and amateurish.

"Where is your wife?"

Percy felt color rising in his face. His mind racing, he stammered, "Oh, uh, she, she was terribly tired after the long drive today and headed back to the hotel ahead of me. We're staying at the Lord Camden Inn up the street. She'll be fine in the morning, I'm sure." He should have stopped talking, knew that he was saying too much, but he couldn't help himself. "We don't eat a lot of clam chowder in Virginia. It may have upset her stomach a little."

"I didn't catch your name, Mister..."

"Hope. Uh, Percy Hope."

"Ok, Mr. Hope. Come on by my office tomorrow morning around ten. Will that work for you?"

"That would be perfect. We saw your office when we walked down here from the hotel. That's what reminded us."

"And I suppose you saw my picture." Dillon was still smiling, actually enjoying Percy's story.

"Your picture?" Percy could feel himself sweating, and could practically hear the saliva drying up in his mouth. Was there a picture in the window of his office?

"Well, of course. Otherwise, how would you have known I was Dillon Harrison?"

Percy felt the air rushing out of the room, felt what the wildebeest must feel right before the jaws of the lion devoured his hindquarters. There was no picture in Harrison's office window, just gold plated lettering. Out of nowhere, Percy formulated a response, "Actually, Mr. Harrison, it was dumb, blind luck. I took a chance. You just looked like a successful lawyer to me!"

Dillon Harrison laughed out loud, not the nervous, faked laughter of a man in trouble, but the honest laughter of a man who appreciates the quick wits of someone who actually is in trouble. "Well, I'm going to take that as a compliment, and I will see you and your wife in the morning."

They shook hands and Percy continued calmly through the door and back to the hotel to meet Beth. Dillon returned to his drink. It would be the first of many.

"But, what about grace?"

Beth was sitting at the little table where the chocolate-cov-
ered strawberries were placed, looking out the balcony door
at the lights running up and down the great masts of the sail
boats on the bay. They should have put the strawberries in
the little refrigerator under the television, but they had left
them out, so now they were sweating and looking old. Beth
ate one anyway. Seeing her father's face for the first time was
an experience she would never forget. Their eyes had met, and
he seemed to know her, even in that instant, even after more
than 30 years, he seemed to know it was her, his child. It had
unsettled her in an unexpected way. She had often wondered
what she would feel at the first glimpse of him. Would there
be any recognition? What emotion would flow to the surface:
anger, resentment, fear? Nothing had prepared her for love.
Her first reaction to seeing the father who had totally abandoned her was an overwhelming desire to run to him. Then, as
surprising and unnerving as her first response had been, soon
after, all was emotional panic. Could she bear it if he didn't
return her love, or worse, treated her with indifference? She
wasn't ready to find out, in a bar, after being on the road for

two days. She had left it to Percy to work out the details of a meeting while she fled out through the kitchen and out the back door. Now she just sat, watching the boats and waiting.

Beth heard the credit card key slide in the slot at the door, and her heart skipped a beat. Percy walked in and headed straight for the gas fireplace and switched it on. A blue flame shot through the fake ceramic logs, then quickly spread out and turned yellow, giving a decent impression of a real fire only without heat.

"Good Lord, I bet the temperature has dropped 20 degrees since we got here."

"Well?" Beth was annoyed with Percy's nonchalance. "Did you talk to him? Did he believe the story?"

"I did talk to him. I'm not sure he believed my story, but nevertheless, we have an appointment at ten tomorrow morning in his office."

"Thank you." Beth struggled to keep her emotions in check, fighting back tears. "Thanks for helping me through this. I just wasn't ready to meet him... in that bar. I just panicked, that's all. Anyway, thank you so much for being there for me."

Percy took off his coat and turned his back to the fire. He didn't want to come on too strong. The last thing she needed to know was how much he was in love with her, still in love with her despite everything. "Don't mention it. It's what ex-husbands are for."

Beth smiled at him and then looked around at the room. Percy anticipated her question. "Yeah, um, this hotel didn't have any suites, yet another reason we should have stayed someplace else. You can take one and I'll take the other. It will be just like Lucy and Desi back in the 50s sleeping in separate beds, only we're not married, so that's really a crappy analogy... and I should probably stop rambling on at this point."

"If I get scared in the night, or start crying, will you reach across the aisle and hold my hand?" It was meant as a throwaway line, and they both briefly laughed, but once the lights were out, it was exactly how they spent the first half hour until Beth finally fell asleep. Percy lay in bed watching the fireplace light flicker across the ceiling. Since the day he had learned the truth about Beth's family, he had been overcome by a desire to protect her. She had so much to lose if the next day didn't go well. Beth was fragile, her confidence as vulnerable to an ill wind as a house of cards. But wasn't it he who had encouraged her to come here? Now, less than 12 hours from the confrontation, Percy was having doubts.

Two long days on the road and the stress of the day finally yielded to sleep that was disturbed abruptly when, at 4:06 on the red digital clock, Percy heard the whistle of a cold wind racing through a gap in the seal of the sliding glass balcony doors. When he walked over to make sure the door was fully latched, he heard the flicker of tiny ice pellets glancing off the glass. He pulled back the curtain enough to see the snow and sleet lashing down in sheets of silver and white all the way down Main Street. He thought it had gotten awfully cold during the evening, and now a storm had come. The wind was chopping the water in the harbor, causing the tall masts to sway back and forth. This was the sort of thing that the people of this town were used to, but in Percy aroused concern. The last thing he wanted was to be snowbound in this town if Dillon Harrison turned out to be an asshole. When he crawled back into bed, Beth was there. He froze in place, unsure how to respond or what to say. Beth broke the silence with a whisper, "Just hold me, Percy. Hold me." Then she turned her back to him and he slid under the covers to her side. Her body was warm, and he held her close. They slept the rest of the night secure in each other's arms while outside the snow and sleet beat against the glass doors.

In the morning, Percy got up, walked to the balcony and looked outside. It had stopped snowing, and the wind was calm. He touched the glass and felt the bitter cold. Beth was still asleep and in the same position she had been in all night, curled up in a ball with the covers stretched to her chin. Percy sat down and watched her sleep. He looked at the night stand clock. 7:30. He thought it best to get his shower out of the way and order room service breakfast before she had awakened. When he got out of the shower she was still out cold. He remembered that she loved French toast with cinnamon. He spoke softly into the phone while ordering breakfast for two. When it arrived, he laid everything out on the balcony window table, poured Beth a cup of black coffee, then sat on the edge of the bed and began rubbing her arm. After a while, she began to stir, then sat up and took the coffee from his hand with a smile. "Thank you." Then she noticed the smell of maple syrup. When she saw the breakfast table in the corner, she reached for Percy's hand. "You're incredible, you know that?"

"Well, I think you need to eat a good breakfast today, and I know how much you love French toast, so..." They both walked over and sat down to eat. Percy pulled back the curtains to reveal the snow, nearly four inches judging by the balcony rail.

"Oh my God!" Beth brought both hands to her mouth. "I dreamed last night that it had snowed! All night I had this dream that we were caught in a blizzard and couldn't find his office."

"Maybe that's why you were hogging the covers. It's stopped now. Snowed like crazy for a few hours, then blew out to sea, I suppose. It looks like the sky is clear."

"Do you think he'll still come into the office in the snow?"

"Beth, this is Maine. Last night I saw two guys wearing shorts and flip flops. To these people it doesn't even qualify as snow unless it's up to the running boards of the trucks. He'll be there."

Beth finished half of her breakfast, then got in the shower. It took her over an hour to get dressed, but when she emerged from the vanity room, she looked like a vision, like a red-haired Grace Kelly in Rear Window, wearing a soft green jacket with matching skirt and her hair pulled back elegantly in the back. Percy caught his breath just at the sight of her.

"What do you think, too much, too dressy? How does one dress at age 35 when meeting one's father for the first time as an adult? I look ridiculous, like I'm trying too hard, right?"

"No, you look like Grace Kelly in Rear Window, and I wouldn't change a thing."

Percy's reassurance settled the matter. They sat at their little table and looked out the window at the now busy street and waited. It was 10:00. They wouldn't want to look too anxious by arriving too early. They sat in silence until Percy thought to ask a procedural question. "How should we begin the conversation?"

Beth, looking gorgeous and surprisingly sedate, reached for his hand and replied, "You've done everything so far just to give me this opportunity. From here on out, let me do the talking."

"Ok. Do you know what you're going to say?"

"No, I don't. But I'm sure it will come to me."

And with that, they put on their coats and rode the elevator to the lobby, braced themselves against the cold and walked the one block up Main Street to the offices of Dillon Harrison, Attorney At Law.

Dillon Harrison had sat at the bar drinking until after midnight when he was encouraged to leave so the closing crew at Cappy's could beat the storm home. Then he stumbled up the street to his office and slept on the sofa in the lunchroom in the back. He awoke at eight with a throbbing headache, brewed himself some coffee, then shoveled away the snow at the entrance to his front door. Then he cleaned himself up in the shower-bath he had installed just off the back wall of his office. He was at least presentable now, and after he brushed his teeth twice and used half a bottle of mouthwash, he didn't smell like a distillery. But there would be no hiding the fact that he had survived a rough night. Now, it was time to sit and wait, and glance through the wooden blinds down the street in the direction of the Lord Camden for a sign of them. What in God's name would he say to her? A bottle of Vodka hadn't provided any insights. Perhaps he wouldn't say much of anything. It's what he would have advised a client to do. Maybe he would just sit there and take his medicine, give no reply, make no excuses, offer no admission of guilt, just try soft, tacit understanding.

Then he saw her crossing the street, looking like an angel. The throbbing in his head intensified, and he began to feel his composure slipping away. He shut the blinds and sat down at his desk, waiting for the door to open. He would let them sit out front for a while until he gathered himself. Finally, he took a deep breath and walked into the lobby with as much confidence as he could muster. "Hello, folks! Sorry, my receptionist is out of state with family for Thanksgiving. Come on into my office." He kept his eyes firmly on Percy, not allowing even a quick look at her. His heart was beating faster, he felt suddenly hot, and the room seemed devoid of oxygen. He quickly sat down and directed his words and thoughts towards Percy. "So, you say you've bought a place on Megunticook? That's where I live! Which property did you buy?"

Beth couldn't take her eyes off this nervous, loud man in the wrinkled shirt. It was an out-of-body experience, if she correctly understood the term. She saw herself in him, noticed the curve of his jaw, the shape of his fingers, the perfect teeth, apparently genetic. To her great relief and astonishment, she felt an otherworldly calm fall down from somewhere, draping itself over her body like heavy dew. Suddenly, she experienced perfect serenity and crystal clarity. She spoke.

"Mister Harrison." The sound of her voice startled him, and he finally looked at her. Percy watched closely for a reaction, his own heart racing. He looked enthralled, like he was gazing at art for the first time. His eyes became wet, but he didn't look away.

"I'm afraid we have gotten this appointment on false pretenses. You see, we haven't bought any property, and we aren't here for legal advice. I'm here to ask you a question. Mister Harrison, do you know who I am?"

The silence was complete. He looked into her eyes for what seemed like 30 seconds without a reply. "Yes. I believe I do."

Calmly, with no hint of accusation, Beth asked, "Who am I?"

"I believe that you're the daughter I walked away from 32 years ago. Are you Elizabeth?" The question had come out like a desperate plea, and her name had caught in his throat.

"Yes, I am. My name is Beth Hope, and this is my ex-husband, Percy."

"I always knew that this day would come, and now that it has, I have no idea what to say to you, Elizabeth. Why are you here? Why now?"

Beth, still calm as a morning lake in springtime, answered in a clear, calm voice. "Both Percy and I have come through some life-changing things over the last few months, and it has forced me into some pretty deep reflection about my life. One of the decisions I made was finding you, meeting my father. Like you, I suppose I knew this day would come, and if you had asked me ten years ago, five years ago, even five months ago what I would say to you, I would have known exactly what I would say. But now that I'm here, everything has changed somehow. I thought that I needed to meet you to demand an explanation of some kind, to find the answer to the question of why you left. See, I've only ever heard my mother's side of the story. But now, sitting here in this office looking at you, it doesn't matter anymore."

"I was 19 when your mother and I divorced. We were both kids. She and I were a huge mistake, but you weren't." A tear traced down his face for the first time.

"I've spent most of my life blaming you for everything that ever went wrong in my life. I didn't tell anyone else about you. Percy didn't even know that you were alive until a week ago, and we were married for 12 years. But inside, in my heart, you were the culprit for my failures as a human being, my all-purpose excuse. That ends today. I think I've just now figured out why I'm here, why I drove all this way, what I need to do. I need to tell you that... I forgive you."

Dillon sat back in his chair, ashen face streaked with tears. He reached in his pocket for a handkerchief and dried his eyes. Then he leaned forward again. "Elizabeth, I'm afraid I can't let you do that."

Beth looked startled. "Why can't you let me forgive you? It's not your decision."

"I'm an attorney, and I have defended many guilty people." Dillon's mood had suddenly changed. "Some of the crimes have been relatively minor, some have been horrific. Sometimes a victim has a change of heart during the trial and decides that he doesn't really want to press charges after all, wants the guilty to get a second chance. But whenever that happens, it's too late. No matter what the victim might feel, it doesn't matter once the guilt has been determined. Justice has to be served. See, Elizabeth, some sins aren't yours to forgive. My sins where you are concerned must be paid in full. Anything good that you have accomplished in your life has come in spite of the terrible hand you were dealt at your birth. I could have changed everything for you, could have given you everything, but it would have required a better man than I was at 19. But the sad thing is, nothing has really changed for me. Although I've had some success, I'm still not man enough to be your father. So, no, you can't just pronounce me forgiven. Life doesn't work that way."

"But, what about grace?"

"That's God's business. Here on Earth, it's about justice."

Percy mostly watched and listened as the two of them talked of philosophy and religion. Hearing Beth make the case for forgiveness and the doctrine of grace was unfathomable to him. Who was this woman? As amazed as he was, Percy was having trouble seeing where everything was headed. What would be the end result of this increasingly bizarre encounter? Here was Beth offering a blanket pardon and Dillon rejecting it on the grounds that he didn't deserve her mercy. As the conversation wore on, Percy noticed a slight shake in Dillon's hands, the whiff of mouthwash-lathered breath, the weariness of his words, like a man who had given up on himself. Then he saw Beth point to the pictures of his family on the credenza behind him.

"Do they know about me?"

"My ex-wife knows about my previous marriage and about a child that was born, that's all. Neither of the twins knows about you, no."

"Can you tell me about them?"

Dillon reached behind him and picked up the most recent photograph of the two of them, one that was taken the night of their college graduation party. "They're both 22, Christopher and Christine, great kids. Chris is in advertising. Chrissy was looking for a husband at school but got a degree in Applied Feminism or some such thing instead, and now lives with her mother trying to discover what she wants to do with her life."

Beth took the picture from him and stared longingly, like a blind person just receiving her sight. She touched the glass with her fingers. Christine was beautiful, with long hair and a radiant smile. "Christine and I look a lot alike."

"It was the first thing I noticed when I saw you walking down the street a while ago. The resemblance is amazing really."

Dillon took the picture back and placed it on the credenza as a disturbing quiet descended upon the room. They all sat amidst the silence, thinking of what could possibly come next. Beth sat leaning forward in expectation; Dillon slumped back against the headrest looking exhausted, the body language a perfect summation, Percy thought, of the last 30 minutes. Finally, Dillon asked the question, "Elizabeth, what is it that you want? What now?"

"I've lived the first 34 years of my life without a father. I think that's long enough. I know that one conversation can't erase the past, but I would like to get to know you, to at least stop pretending that you don't exist."

Percy had never seen a man look more defeated, more devastated than Dillon Harrison at that moment. His eyes lowered and his voice seemed barely above a whisper, "You may not like what you discover."

"I'm willing to take that chance." Beth's smile was warm, her expression exultant, as though she had witnessed a breakthrough. The contrast produced in Percy's heart a foreboding sense of darkness, a fleeting wave of nausea that passed when Beth walked around the desk and threw her arms around her father. Dillon physically stiffened, then briefly reciprocated more out of awkward obligation than genuine affection. For Percy, the entire scene was accompanied by an unexplainable sadness. As they exchanged numbers and made promises to call each other and maybe plan another visit, Percy smiled and hoped.

◇ **18** ◇

Red Light Nightmare

The rest of the day was magical for Beth. She became suddenly fascinated with everything about Camden. The town had made an amazingly fast recovery from the four inches of snow that would have had every town in Virginia paralyzed. The roads were plowed, the sidewalks cleared, and everything was open for business by the time they walked out of Dillon's office. Every shop seemed to delight her. They walked through each one, sampling fudge here and taffy there. There were small art galleries, antique stores, and lots of hand-crafted Maine jewelry featuring bright gemstones set in elaborately elegant earrings and bracelets. For Percy it was very much like being married again, except for the fact that Beth wasn't at all interested in buying anything. She seemed to be enchanted by the beauty of everything she touched, as if it was the very first time she had ever held anything so fine, fresh and new.

By the time the sun began to set, they were leaning back in two comfortable chairs in the Camden Library, getting warm. Beth reached for Percy's hand. "I think that this might very well be the best day of my life."

Percy smiled and gave her freezing cold fingers a squeeze.

"And you didn't even buy anything."

"That's right! I didn't even buy a thing." Beth's face was alive with wonder, and if it were even possible, she looked five years younger than she had that morning. "What in the world has happened to me Percy?"

Percy looked into her eyes, saw the pure joy there, and wondered the exact same thing. He wanted desperately to feel happy, deliriously happy for her, but couldn't fight off the dark image of Dillon from earlier that had shaken him. But now, looking at Beth and seeing the transformation, he would have to shake it off somehow. "I have to admit, I've never seen you like this. I'm also pretty sure that you've never been so beautiful than you are right now, at this moment."

Suddenly, the old mischief was back in her eyes. "You're only saying that because you finally got me inside a library."

"Not very long ago, you and I couldn't even speak a civil word to one another. Now, look at us." Percy could hardly believe how rapidly things had changed, how dramatically the terrain between them had been transformed. It was dizzying.

"Aurelius was right. Fate has brought us together, twice in one lifetime."

Percy was momentarily confused to hear Beth make reference to Marcus Aurelius. Never in a million years could he imagine her reading his words. A memory flashed through his mind; hadn't she quoted that particular line in one of his dreams? The memory vanished. He was overwhelmed with the moment. His questions and fears melted away as she jumped out of her chair. "I'm starving. Where shall we go for dinner?"

The librarian suggested Peter Ott's and insisted that they have gingerbread for dessert. As they walked down Main Street and got closer to Dillon's office, Beth wondered whether they should ask him if he wanted to join them. Percy had cautioned against it on the grounds that it might be too much for one day. As they passed, the office was closed anyway. Still, Beth stopped and looked through the windows, saying nothing.

Peter Ott's was one of those strange buildings in Maine that looked big on the outside but felt small once you walked in, small but not cramped. The meal was delicious, and the dessert recommendation was superb. As they were drinking their coffee, Percy was wondering what it would be like to make love to Beth after so long a time. Would it complicate the moment, or would it be the natural conclusion to this, the most momentous day of their lives?

Percy sat and listened to Beth talk about every thought that entered her mind, a flood of extemporaneous expression, newly freed from some place inside where she had stored them up all of her life. She didn't know what to call Dillon. "Dad" seemed too familiar and unearned. "Mister Harrison" seemed too formal. She wished so much that her friend and therapist, Melinda, were here to share the moment with her. She had been so right about the power of forgiveness. She could never possibly repay Percy for being with her, standing beside her, encouraging her to take the chance. Then she suddenly became serious. She began reciting a list of her failures as a wife and as a person. She began explaining how wrong she had been, how unfairly she had dealt with him, and how much she had hurt the only man she had ever loved. Then she talked of the changes she had made, the power of her new faith, the miracle that had been worked because of grace and forgiveness. Then she asked if he could possibly forgive her and give her another chance to make it up to him. It was all too much for Percy. "You act as though you're the only one of us who failed in our marriage. There were plenty of times when I was a complete asshole to you, Beth."

"Yes, I agree, but this isn't a competition, Percy. We were both at fault, but I need for you to forgive me. Do you think you can, or have I just hurt you too deeply for us to ever find our way again?"

"Yes, I can forgive you. The reason I can is that I'm still in love with you. But forgiving is one thing, living with you and starting over together is another. The idea scares me, to tell the truth. You scare me a little, Beth. Don't get me wrong, you're amazing, a delight. You're almost like a dream to me, but I need something more than a dream. I'm not sure I could survive losing you a second time."

They sat in silence for a while, thinking things through, taking inventory of each other's words, trying to find a way forward. Finally, Percy called for the check, paid it, and they walked back to the hotel through the cold, still night.

This time it was Beth who turned on the gas fireplace and held her hands against its suggestion of heat. Both of them began to feel the expectation of the moment. Percy took off his coat and walked over behind Beth, rubbing the outside of her arms with his hands. She leaned her head back against his shoulder and they stood still for a while watching the fire.

Like so much of their life together, sex between them had always been a frenzied thing, filled with energy and passion, a tinderbox of erotica sparked by the slightest and most unexpected provocation. There had always been a manic quality to their lovemaking, a frenetic athleticism, as if sex was something that had to be done as if for the last time. They were the only couple they knew who didn't think that Hollywood sex was unrealistic, what with couples tearing each other's clothes off before they had hardly entered the house, with not the slightest hint of modesty. For most of their friends, this sort of depiction of sex was unrecognizable, even laughable. For Percy and Beth, it was more like Wednesday night. But like everything else between them lately, this too seemed dramatically changed. As they held each other in front of the fire, there was a moment of recognition when they both knew what was about to happen, but if anything, that understanding seemed to slow them down. They came together with a newfound tenderness, a more gentle touch, love more accurately timed with an hourglass than a stopwatch. When they lay still afterwards, there was finally a sense of safety, of contentment, and then sleep overtook them both, deep and peaceful. Outside, silence fell over the town of Camden, Maine.

Just like the night before, Beth dreamed of snow, sheets of white coming down in waves; the wind making howling noises that echoed around her, glancing off unseen walls through the blizzard. She stumbled along, lost and confused, trudging forward through the storm. In the distance, there was a red light, haloed by the white and silver of the snow. It seemed to be pulsing, waxing and waning in strength. Beth felt compelled to push through to the light, but the faster she gave chase, the more distant the light became. It was a maddening and pointless pursuit that left her drained and angry. When the dream finally ended, she woke up with a start, covered in sweat. It took a few seconds for her to be sure it was truly over. She was disoriented and confused. She slid out of bed, careful not to wake Percy, walked over to the balcony doors, and slowly pulled back the curtains. The street below was clear, the sky above was dazzled by a million stars. She took a deep breath and felt a little silly for even checking. She looked down Main Street towards her father's office. It was still there, its smart royal blue awning lit up by the soft streetlamps. Beth drank a glass of water and then got back in bed. Percy was awake and waiting for her. They made love again, then fell asleep in each other's arms, their room bathed in moonlight streaming through the opened curtains of the balcony.

At dawn, Percy's eyes opened slowly. The memories of the night came to him, and he turned quickly towards Beth in a panic, thinking that it may all have been a dream. But there she was, her red hair flowing across her pillow, sound asleep, looking to Percy like everything he had ever wanted in his life. He kissed her hair and was sliding closer to her when he noticed the reflected red light racing across the ceiling over his head. He watched it for a minute, confused and lethargic, not wanting to have to leave Beth's side to go investigate, but after a while he realized that he had left the balcony curtains open in the night. He quietly slipped out of bed and reached up to close them when his eyes caught a glimpse of what looked like a police car's flashing light on Main Street below. He rubbed his eyes and then refocused, noticing that it was several pairs of lights. There were actually several vehicles sitting at odd angles in the street, a couple of police cars and an ambulance all directly in front of... Dillon's office.

The darkness returned in an instant, bleak and terrifying, shaking Percy. He closed the curtains, blocking the lights and sounds from entering the room. A thousand chaotic thoughts raced through his head. He had to find out what was happening. He must protect Beth. It might be nothing; it might not have anything to do with Dillon. So, why was his heart pounding? Why was he so overcome by fear? He looked at Beth, totally and completely at peace. He found his pants, put on his shoes, threw on a jacket and wrote a quick note to Beth in case she woke up before he returned, telling her that he was out picking up a newspaper and some bagels for breakfast. Then he raced down the hallway, ran down the stairs and out into the street. He ran towards the noise and lights. By now there was a crowd of people gathered at the sight. Percy recognized the bartender from Cappy's. There was yellow police tape up and down the sidewalk around Dillon's office and a large officer with a State trooper's hat talking on a cell phone out in the street. Percy felt as if his life was slipping away from him, a painful hole in his stomach began to ache in anticipation of horrible news. Percy caught the eye of the bartender and asked, "What happened here?"

"I think there's been a shooting. I think Dillon Harrison is dead, killed himself early this morning; least that's what I picked up on my scanner."

$\diamond$ **19** $\diamond$

A Green Metal Box

Brilliant sunshine splashed every car on the road with sparkling light, making them all seem clean and new. The sky was a cloudless blue from the minute they had left Camden, all the way home. But, it had been nearly a wordless trip, an interminable, silent wake. Beth stared blankly out of the window. Percy could never find appropriate music; everything was either too spirited or too somber. Every attempt to start a conversation had been either ignored or politely killed by inattention. Beth had eaten little, and Percy was starting to worry that he might be losing her again, that perhaps she blamed him for encouraging her to make this ill-fated trip in the first place. Percy certainly did. The hardest part was not knowing, the stifling silence.

When he had come back to the room to tell her, she had collapsed in his arms and clung to him through it all. The police had questioned them, since they had been the last people to see him in his office. Dillon had left no note, no explanation for the decision to shoot himself through the roof of his mouth with a 12-gauge shotgun, spraying the top half of his head onto the wall behind his credenza, covering his family photos in a fine grey mist. Throughout, Beth had hung tightly on Percy's arm. They had made the decision not to attend the funeral, not wanting to risk an encounter with Dillon's family. Once the decision to leave Camden had been made, Beth had withdrawn. The crying was over, the tears had stopped, and she had retreated behind a wall of silence.

Percy had decided to make the drive straight through, not wanting the awkwardness of a hotel room. They had stopped at a Denny's in New Jersey for a dinner of pancakes and coffee, then Percy had driven on through the night while Beth slept. The 13-hour journey ended around midnight when Percy pulled into the driveway of what had once been his dream house. As Percy removed Beth's luggage from the back, he wondered what he should do. Should he leave her alone for the night? Should he offer to stay in the guestroom? What was the protocol now between them? So much had happened over the past week it was impossible to know.

A package with a UPS sticker was leaned up against the front door. Beth picked it up and walked inside. After turning on the lights she could see that the package was sent to "Elizabeth Hope" from a Camden address. Beth searched the package for a shipment date and found it, the day that Dillon had killed himself. "Percy," Beth's voice was weak and trembling, "this is from Dillon."

Percy took the package from her hands and looked it over. "Do you want to open it now, or would you rather wait until morning? It's been a very long day."

"No. Open it now."

Percy sliced the crease of the box with his truck key, then removed the heavy green metal box and sat it on the coffee table. The key had been taped to the lid. Beth sat down beside him as he opened the box. The two of them would remain on the sofa, sorting through its contents until daylight.

It was the story of her life stacked chronologically from the impression of her feet as an infant to a real estate ad with her picture as the listing agent. There were photographs from the Diamondback, the student newspaper at the University of Maryland, her engagement announcement, her wedding picture from the Times-Dispatch, along with a clip reporting the issuance of a building permit to Percy and Beth Hope. They both caught their breath when they saw the black and white photograph of their house. The landscapers were laying out the sod of the front lawn. The picture was taken from down the street. Dillon had been here, what was that, ten years ago? He had come here and taken a picture of their house and never even left a note.

The effort taken to gather each of these artifacts from the life he had never lived, the obsession that had never waned, right up to the cutting out of Gilbert and Frances' obituary, and never one communication, never a single note, never one phone call. Even in this, his final act, there was no explanation attached, just the accumulated treasure of Beth's life in a green metal box. He had taken the box down the street to the UPS store and had it shipped here just hours before killing himself. Beth was numbed by the staggering selfishness of it, the thoughtlessness, the cruelty of such an act. Tears flowed down her cheeks from some strange place, for she no longer felt any compassion for her father, just an overwhelming disgust. Exhausted, she lay back against the sofa and fell asleep just as the sunlight began streaming through the windows.

Percy placed everything gently back inside the box, draped a blanket over Beth and watched her sleep. How could he possibly have done such a thing? How could his own anguish have become so overpowering, so hopeless? How could he not have thought of those he would leave behind, and what would become of their lives? How could he have launched himself off that bridge three years ago? What would his parents have done without him? Now, he looked at Beth asleep beside him and wondered how she would recover from such a blow, after having her hopes lifted so high and then crushed in such a violent and merciless way. Despite having spent over thirteen hours on the road and the past four hours in agony over Dillon's box, Percy knew that sleep would not come. He lifted Beth and took her upstairs into her bed, then walked downstairs and made himself some coffee. He looked at the clock in the kitchen. Eight o'clock. He decided that he would stay until she woke up and take it from there.

Beth's cell phone rang at 8:30. It had startled him since he had never heard it ring before. Apparently, Beth didn't give out her number to many people. Percy didn't even know it. The sound came from her purse, which was on the floor at his feet. The screen said, "Melinda." Percy let it ring a couple more times before deciding to answer. When she heard his voice, she asked if he was Percy. She said that the suspense had been killing her, and since it had been several days, she thought she would call. She knew about the trip; she knew about Beth's father. She seemed to know quite a lot about everything. Percy didn't feel right about sharing the details, thinking that it was something she needed to hear directly from Beth. He did say that it hadn't gone well and that Beth would need her help dealing with everything. He told her that Beth had spoken highly of her; he spoke of how grateful he was personally for her influence in Beth's life. He found himself warming to her in just a few minutes of a cell phone conversation. He promised to tell Beth that she had called. He placed the phone back in her purse and finished his coffee.

Beth slept until two o'clock in the afternoon. Percy fixed her lunch, and they ate together in silence.

"Melinda called this morning. Your cell phone rang. I saw her name, so I answered. She wanted to know how you were. She sounds nice."

"What did you tell her?"

"Nothing really. I said that it was a difficult trip and that she should call you again later today. I thought it was something that she should hear from you."

Finally, a spark of emotion. "And how will that conversation go? So, yeah, Melinda, I finally met my father after 30 years. Come to find out, he's been secretly stalking me my entire life, but once he finally gets to actually meet me face to face, it takes him less than 24 hours to blow his brains out."

Percy wanted to object, wanted to point out how complex a thing suicide was, how no one event was to blame, that it was more a warehouse full of small things that had led Dillon to kill himself. But he couldn't form the words and instead responded, "I'm so sorry, Beth. I just don't know what to say to you."

"That's because there isn't anything to say."

Percy gathered up the dishes and put them in the dishwasher. He busied himself in the kitchen while he thought of how to approach the subject of the immediate future. How were he and Beth to live in this new and fragile world? Now was the worst time to bring up the subject, but it was hanging in the air around them. Percy's luggage was still in the truck, he hadn't slept in what felt like days, but he needed some guidance, some clarification of their status.

"Listen, Beth. I know that this is a terrible time for this discussion. You've been through hell, and we're both exhausted. But I was wondering about... us. I'm not sure what the right thing is now. I don't want to leave you alone, but I'm not sure I should be here. I could stay in the guestroom if you like, or I could just leave and give you a few days. Or we could stay together... forever." He regretted the words as soon as they had come out of his mouth. What an idiotic thing to say at a time like this! "I'm sorry, that was stupid of me to say. What I mean is, I don't want to leave you alone, but I also don't want to complicate things for you either. I'll do whatever you think is best."

"What I think is best." Beth lifted the metal box from the coffee table and sat it in her lap. "I don't know what's best. You're all I have left, Percy, but I need some time to myself,

I think. I don't know. Maybe you should make the decision. I don't trust my judgment right now."

And that was that. Percy had moved back home, back to 16 Jennings Lane. He had promised to look in on her, and she had given him her cell phone number. He told her that he loved her. She had walked him to his truck and kissed him before he left, then stood in the driveway and watched his truck disappear.

◇ **20** ◇

Regeneration

He would give her as much time as she needed. He would throw himself into his work with new enthusiasm. Exams came and went. Christmas came and went. The days turned into weeks, then months. They went on dates occasionally, had dinner at Harry's a few times. They started out talking on the phone a lot, then, with time, the calls got shorter and less frequent. After a while Beth had stopped calling altogether. Percy had asked for an explanation, and she had said that she just wasn't ready, she needed more time, and she wasn't sure how much, and honestly didn't know if she would ever be ready.

The words had wounded Percy, cut him deeply. He asked her if she blamed him for urging her to make contact with her father, and she assured him that it wasn't like that at all. She would always be grateful for his support, but maybe the only way she would ever be able to get past it all was by making a fresh start. Percy asked if she was seeing someone else. She said no. She wanted them to remain friends. Percy reminded her that they had never been friends in the first place, they had always either been lovers or haters, passionately married or bitterly divorced. Beth said that a part of her would always love him and that she could never bring herself to hate him ever again, and why couldn't they just try being friends? But as soon as they parted ways, Beth never made much of an effort at friendship, and neither did Percy. They had simply turned each other loose to find out what life would be like apart.

Beth went back to work selling homes. It kept her busy and focused. She began getting more involved with Dave and Melinda and their church, making friends with people with whom she had nothing in common, nothing except a nascent and fragile faith. Every man in the church who wasn't married was in love with her, but their attentions embarrassed her. The last thing that Beth was interested in was another relationship. She cared about one thing and one thing only, her determined effort to become a better person, what Dave called "regeneration." The hardest doctrine for Beth to accept was the strange notion that salvation could not be earned, that it was a free gift. One night in an open discussion with 15 or so people at Melinda's apartment, Beth had blurted out, "My experience in life has been that whenever you're offered free anything, it either comes with strings attached, or it's not worth a damn to start with! Free means second rate, cheap, and besides, anything worth having in this life costs you something."

It was one of the things that so endeared Beth to Melinda. She didn't know the language of faith and questioned every assumption she confronted with candor and honesty. The questions she asked were penetrating, sometimes sharp-edged and coarse. But they came from a place of authentic yearning, a very personal and all-consuming quest for truth. Melinda and Beth had continued their sessions together, but after a while she stopped charging since they had become such good friends and were constantly spending time together anyway; it didn't seem right. Beth spoke with Melinda about every detail of her life, holding back nothing, even her most despicable thoughts. Soon their bond was unbreakable.

Percy spent the first few days after his final conversation with Beth in suffering anguish. His dreams of a life with Beth had died and there had been nothing to take its place. What he had desired from life had always been centered around Beth, and now that she wasn't there, he only had books, music and a job teaching 13th grade at a community college. After allowing himself a week to wallow in self pity, he had made an appointment with Dr. Kennedy. Several sessions later he was over the worst of it and began to give serious consideration to what exactly he wanted to do with the rest of his life. The only things he had ever really loved to do were read and gamble, neither a reliable money maker, except, that wasn't exactly true. He had only lost money gambling one time, when he was unstable, half out of his mind with grief over losing Beth. Before that, gambling had been golden. Maybe now that Beth was out of his life for good, his gift would return. He didn't really need the money, but the money wouldn't hurt. It would be a while before a decent university would hire him any-way. Winning had been a huge thrill, and that was something in short supply for Percy Hope. He could use a thrill or two. When the last spring exam was over, Percy planned a trip to Atlantic City.

The first week of April, Melinda had surprised Beth one night by showing up at the house unannounced, to break the news that she was pregnant. It had come as a big surprise since neither Dave nor Melinda had planned on starting a family just yet, but now that it was done, they were both thrilled by the news. Beth surprised herself by crying. Melinda was prob-ably the best friend she had ever had, and to see her so happy, so delighted to be on the cusp of such a grand adventure was overpowering. It suddenly occurred to Beth that in all of her life, she had never before been so overjoyed by someone else's happiness. "This must be what friendship feels like," Beth thought as she listened to Melinda's story about the preg-nancy test turning blue and how she had broken the news to Dave and his reaction.

As the weeks marched by, Beth helped Melinda decorate the tiny nursery in their ridiculously small apartment, went shopping for baby clothes with her, and marveled at the way Dave treated her with renewed tenderness and care. If it was even possible, being pregnant had made Melinda even more giving, more caring, more compassionate than before.

One night Beth was watching a movie at their apartment. It wasn't a very good one and Dave and Beth kept talking over the dialogue, making fun of the actors. Out of nowhere, Dave asked Beth, "Tell me, why exactly did you break things off with Percy?"

Beth glanced at Melinda, then back at Dave with a shy smile on her face, wondering where on earth that question had come from. Dave continued, "I'm just curious, that's all. There are probably a dozen guys at church who are out of their minds about you, and you won't give any of them the time of day."

"Well, I'm clearly a lesbian," Beth replied before throwing a handful of popcorn across the room at him. Melinda laughed hysterically and threw a handful of her own. After things settled down, they began watching the movie again, and Beth congratulated herself on dodging the question. Only, the question rattled around in her head for the rest of the night, accusing and unanswered.

Beth drove home in silence, no radio, no music, just the hum of the tires on the pavement, thinking about that first weekend at the Borgata, Percy standing under that vast chandelier in his UVA sweatshirt, so casual and unhurried, the graceful way he walked, so completely in command of himself. But Beth had only noticed the grace of his walk after he had been identified as the luckiest man in America, the type of introduction that tended to smooth out rough edges. So much of the weekend seemed a blur to her now, but the memories that had survived were especially vivid. She remembered the incredible calm that would come over him whenever he was about to play for high stakes, the steadiness of his hands, how he never once looked nervous or ill at ease. She remembered the long night at the blackjack table when he had won hand after hand while revealing not one trace of emotion, his demeanor never wavering as his winnings piled up. From the look of him, one couldn't tell whether he was $10,000 up or down. He gambled like a man who knew he couldn't lose, and yet had managed to stay within himself, displaying his talents judiciously so as not to attract too much attention.

It had been at that table that night, watching his gift on full display, that Beth had decided that he would be hers. Love had never entered into her calculations. If love somehow came later that would be a bonus. Beth had fallen hook, line, and sinker, not for Percy, but for his gift and the power it had to transform her life, to elevate her above the rabble, to rescue her from the mediocre life that lay in front of her. Beth knew that she had the tools to make it happen; she knew it from the moment she had kissed him.

He was hesitant, shy, and she could feel him shaking slightly when he placed his hand on the small of her back. He had never been kissed by someone like her, someone saucy, aggressive and hot. Girls like Beth had been unapproachable to guys like Percy, who, although not at all unattractive, still lacked that peculiar cut of the jaw, the smooth, perfectly proportioned facial features, the deep penetrating eyes, and effortless hair that set certain men apart from others. Percy was destined to marry a perfectly lovely girl somewhere, about whom everyone would say that she had made a beautiful bride. But men like Percy never ended up with women like Beth, about whom everyone would say had taken everyone's breath away with her stunning beauty as she floated down the aisle. Percy had his gift and Beth had hers, and on that very first weekend she would use hers to relentless effect. Taking Percy to bed and ensuring he fell in love with her had been an effortless breeze. In 48 short hours, Beth had changed her life forever.

Beth pulled into the driveway and shut off the car. She leaned back against the headrest and thought about Dave's question. The answer was simple. The girl Percy had fallen in love with hadn't been worth it. He deserved better. He deserved the woman she was determined to become.

◇ 21 ◇

The Letter

The letter had come overnight from Federal Express and had been leaned against her front door sometime during the day. Beth had placed it on the kitchen counter along with the other mail of the day, kicked off her heels, gotten a bottle of water from the fridge and settled down on the sofa. She didn't recognize the sender's address. She pulled on the tab and slowly ripped an opening in the envelope.

Dear Mrs. Hope,

It has taken me a long time to find the courage to write this letter. Almost six months ago my father took his own life. Needless to say it came as quite a shock to all of us. He left no note of explanation. Trying to determine his motivations has been a very trying process, and I'm not sure we will ever know what was in his mind that awful night. My dad divorced my mother several years ago, and I have lived with her ever since, but I still had a good relationship with him and loved him very much.

Since his death I have discovered that you and your husband were the last people to see him in his office. In addition, I have come across information that leads me to believe that your appointment with my dad was of a personal nature. The information I have discovered suggests that you might have known my dad for many years. I hope you don't think me too presumptuous, but it's very important for me to find out why my dad chose to end his life, and if you can shed any light on his state of mind that night it would be appreciated more than you know.

My brother and I will be traveling to Richmond in a couple of weeks and would very much like to visit you and discuss this in more detail. We will be in Richmond for two days, Thursday and Friday of next week. If you will agree to see us, please write a time that is convenient for you on the enclosed card and return it to us in the postage-paid envelope I have provided.

Thank you and I hope to see you soon.

Sincerely,

Christine Harrison

Beth read the letter a second time and then a third, hoping that it would make more sense the more she read it, that the words would seem less threatening, less accusing. She wanted to call Percy, but she hadn't called him for weeks now, she would be using him, and she didn't want to hurt him any deeper than she already had. Maybe she could call Melinda. Against her better judgment, she found herself in her car driving to Percy's house, then pulling into the driveway right next to the truck. She rang the doorbell, but nobody answered. Then she smelled steak cooking on the grill around back. She walked around the bright pink azalea bushes, which had just burst forth in full bloom. She stopped short when she saw Percy throwing a tennis ball from the deck all the way to the end of the yard where the huge pines stood in a row. The dog appeared, galloping at full throttle through the yard, past the pines and scooped up the ball, sending a flurry of grass and dirt flying into the air. "Atta-boy Sam!!" Percy was laughing and clapping his hands. "Now, bring it back to me boy. We can't play this game if you won't bring the ball back to me!"

Soon, Sam tired of playing keep-away and ran back to the deck, dropping the ball at Percy's feet. "Good dog! Good Sam!" Percy jostled the dog's ears with both hands, looking totally thrilled with his new friend. Beth stood around the corner, out of sight for a few more minutes, watching the two of them and listening to Percy speaking this new playful tongue, so full of childish formulations and unbridled enthusiasm. At one point she heard him say, "You are daddy's good boy, Sam, yes you are!" It was so strange to hear him speak this way, strange and endearing. Beth hesitated; wondering if this was the right time to walk back into Percy's life, out of the blue, with another fire for him to put out. But she had come this far and couldn't hide behind the forsythia bushes forever. She walked slowly around the corner. "Hi, Percy. I rang the door-bell but nobody answered, but then I heard your voice back here."

Percy stopped dead in his tracks at the sound of her voice. Sam dropped the ball from his mouth and ran down the deck steps to greet her. Beth began patting his head with both hands. "Hello, Sam. Remember me?" she asked, hoping to start a light conversation while she came up with an excuse why she had suddenly appeared in Percy's back yard after three months of nothing.

"Hey Beth." Percy sounded glad to see her, not annoyed or suspicious. "You look nice."

"You too." Beth couldn't look into his eyes very long with-out feeling guilty for hurting him, so she pivoted to every-thing Sam. "So, he sure is a cutie. I stood around the corner earlier, watching the two of you playing with the ball. I think you've made quite a friend there. I assume you've had him all checked out by a vet, right?"

"Yep. I went out a few weeks ago to buy him a dog bed. I'm afraid he'll run off if I let him sleep outside. He already has once. I think he's so used to roaming around, I better keep him inside until I can get a fence built. Yeah. It's been a long time since I've had a dog and I had forgotten how much I enjoy them. Besides, now that I've spent all this money and put all this work into him, I don't want him to just wander off."

"No. You wouldn't want that." Beth felt suddenly very sad and uncomfortable, trapped in the wrong place at the wrong time. She felt she was about to cry when Percy surprised her with an invitation to eat dinner with him and Sam at the table on the deck. "If you haven't eaten, there are three steaks grilling. I've got plenty." Percy looked down at Sam. "Even Sam wants you to stay. Please?"

Beth helped Percy set the table, then sat on the sliding swing. Sam quickly pounced onto the seat beside her and laid his head in her lap. Beth began patting him on the head and wondering how on earth either of them had ended up in Percy's back yard. The meal passed quickly, sped along by idle small talk, Percy asking Beth about the real estate business, and Beth asking Percy why he had started back to church. It was all quite pleasant, two old friends catching up.

After dinner, Beth helped clean up the dishes, then they settled down on the loveseat in the library. Beth removed a book off the seat before sitting down, The Gallic Wars, by Julius Caesar, and handed it to Percy. "So, are you still reading these dusty old history books?"

"I'm afraid so." Percy seemed embarrassed, like a boy caught with a Playboy magazine. "It's an old habit that's hard to break. The ancient Romans have always fascinated me. Haven't you ever wanted to go back in time?"

It wasn't the sort of question she expected from Percy, but she knew the answer with stone cold certainly. While Percy was thinking about the ancient Romans or having dinner with Beethoven and Thomas Jefferson, Beth was thinking about a shorter trip, back to the night they had met at the Borgata. She wanted to be able to find enough courage to answer the question honestly, to say, "Yes, Percy. I wish I could relive our first weekend together. I wish I hadn't known about your gift before I met you. I wish I hadn't been such a manipulative slut, and I wish I had another chance to meet you for the first time." Instead, she just smiled and listened to him go on and on about the fascinating Romans. Then the conversation lagged, and Percy broke the silence with a question Beth did expect, "Why did you come here tonight?"

"I came here because I got a letter in the mail that I wanted to show you because it scared me, and the first thing I always do when I'm afraid is come running to you for help, it seems."

"What the hell are you talking about? When have you ever come running to me for anything? I should be so lucky." Percy's voice was stern, and he sounded irritated.

"Just a few months ago when I found my father on the internet, for one."

"Ok, maybe once, but I wouldn't call that 'running.' You were just asking my opinion about something terrible from your past that I should have been told about long before then. But I wouldn't call that 'running.' Besides, if you're not going to come to me with something like that, who would you go to?"

"But that's just it, Percy. You don't owe me anything anymore. Whatever debt you ever owed me has been paid in full by the roof over my head. I'm not worth one more lost night's sleep." Beth found herself practically screaming, with tears in her eyes.

"Do you have the letter with you?" Percy was calm and in complete control of his emotions. Beth stared at him through her tears, then reached into her purse and handed him the letter. Percy got up from the loveseat and walked over to his desk, sat down in his Herman Miller chair and turned on the desk lamp. He read the letter in silence, got up, and returned to her side on the loveseat.

"So, why does this letter frighten you?"

"It reads like a veiled accusation, like she wants to find a way to blame my visit for his death. The reason it scares me is that she's probably right."

"We've already had this conversation, Beth, so I'm not going to explain how ridiculous that accusation is." Percy didn't want an argument, and neither did Beth, so they both retreated into silence for a while.

"What are you going to do?"

"What do you think I should do?"

"Well, they still think that you and I are married, so as your husband, I would advise you to meet with them. I'll be there with you, and we will tell them everything we know. Then we will listen to them tell us what they know. All three of you have one thing in common; all of you lost your father. Who knows, maybe a connection will be made between you. There's a chance that this could turn out to be a blessing, a beginning of something."

Beth looked at Percy in amazement. How could he be so calm, so levelheaded and logical? Why, after everything, did he still love her?

"You're not actually my husband, you know. So, I don't have to listen to your advice."

"You never listened to my advice when I *was* your husband." Percy smiled and reached for her hand. "Just so you don't think I'm some pathetic push-over, my help with this meeting will come with some serious strings attached."

Beth saw the playfulness return to his eyes and couldn't help smiling. "Oh really? What sort of strings?"

"Now that you're going to church every Sunday, you are no doubt aware that as my wife, you have certain responsibilities, wifely duties, so to speak. It's all right there in Ephesians, I think. So, I'm thinking that since we will be pretending to be married while they are here, I probably should move in a few days before they show up. I mean, you wouldn't want me stumbling into the furniture, would you?"

"What wifely duties are you referring to?"

"Oh, you know, doing my laundry, fixing my meals, letting

Sam sleep in the guestroom, sexual favors on demand, those sorts of things."

"And all of that is in the Bible?"

"Right there in the Holy Book."

"In Ephesians, you say?"

"Yes, I believe so."

"Well, I suppose three out of four isn't too bad."

"Don't worry; I was just joking about the sexual favors!"

"That's too bad. I was going to say; no way is Sam sleeping in the guestroom."

◆ **22** ◆

The Twins

The table was set for four, the first time that had happened in years, Beth thought as she scurried around the room picking at the flower arrangements. Percy was out on the patio warming up the grill. He hadn't moved in, but had been over almost every night for the past week, turning himself into an indispensable man. It had been his idea to invite the Harrison twins for dinner. He had volunteered to grill the London broil; he had suggested everyday dishes instead of china, sweet tea instead of wine, saying that it was vital not to appear too anxious, too pretentious. Fine china would be trying way too hard. It wasn't a celebration, or someone's birthday, it was a first meeting with her half-sister and half-brother who very well might think she was responsible for their father's death. But everything was going to be alright because Percy said so.

Despite the dark cloud of the meeting off in the distance, it had been a great week. Beth had spent almost all of her time with Percy, either at his place, getting to know Sam, or at her place watching movies and having talks that didn't end until after midnight. One night they were both bored with watching Blazing Saddles for the hundredth time, when Beth blurted out, "Why haven't you seen anyone else?"

"Who says I haven't?"

"It's a small town, Percy. You haven't dated anyone since we divorced. Why?"

"Sam and I have been seeing an awful lot of each other lately. Does that count?"

"I'm serious Percy. You're smart, attractive, and I've never heard anyone say a bad word about you. I don't get it."

Percy put a packet of popcorn in the microwave, shut the door and pressed "start." The light inside came on and the package began to travel in short, slow circles. He felt uncomfortable with the question and had tried to laugh his way out of it, but Beth hadn't let it go.

"If you'll remember, my life wasn't exactly smooth sailing after the divorce. I wasn't well, obviously. I guess I found myself dealing with one big scary thing after another there for a while, so dating was never a priority. I just wasn't interested in going down that road again so soon after... everything."

The first scattered kernels began to pop. Then the bag began to bulge in the middle, little breaths of steam rushing out along the edges. Percy pretended to be fascinated, while finishing the conversation with, "Besides, for me, I figured it was either you or nothing."

It was the closest they had come all week to discussing what was to become of them and their relationship. His words had moved her, but she could find no appropriate reply, so she had dropped the subject and they had both returned to the sofa just in time to hear the last line of Hedley Lamarr's speech to his army of thugs as they prepared to destroy Rock Ridge. Percy and Beth recited the words along with him, "Now, go do that voo-doo that you do so well!"

The next night Beth had taken Percy over to meet Dave and Melinda. There was Chinese take-out and lots of talk of pregnancy cravings and not much of religion, which had been a tremendous relief to Percy, who, although very grateful for Melinda's benign influence in Beth's life, wasn't comfortable talking about faith. Melinda had greeted him with a warm hug and announced his arrival with, "So this is the great and good Percy Hope!" Percy hadn't known what to make of it. Was she being sarcastic? But as the night wore on he realized it had been a sincere compliment, an acknowledgment of the high regard with which Beth held him, a comforting thought. Percy had liked Dave almost instantly. Dave had an affable directness, a quick and at times blistering wit. As Percy observed his easy manner, it was easy to forget that he was a minister. Maybe Dave was the "before" to Riggs' "after." Maybe Dave was what preachers were like before 40 years of grappling with the mystery of eternal security had robbed them of their sense of humor.

The only serious topic of the night had been the upcoming meeting with the Harrisons. Percy had felt relief to be able to get someone else's perspective, to see the thing from someone else's eyes. Both Dave and Melinda agreed that Percy's dinner idea was a good one. As Melinda shared her thoughts, Percy could instantly see why Beth raved about her so. Perhaps it was just the maternal glow he had heard so many rumors about, but there was something about Melinda's face that calmed your worst impulses. She was so full of light and optimism, her eyes were alive with some sort of glorious expectation, as if she knew the future and it was going to be great.

"I can't help thinking that this meeting is part of God's plan for you, Beth," she began. "They are both heartbroken over their dad's death, looking for answers, trying to find meaning. And you're just as heartbroken, but for a different reason. For you, your grief is about the future, what might have been. For them it's about what was and will never be again; it's about their memories. For you it's about the memories that you will never have. Think of the powerful healing that could result from such a meeting. After Friday night, you will have a new brother and sister. The possibilities are so exciting!"

Percy had felt obligated to insert some reality, to point out a possible counter narrative if for no other reason than to lessen such lofty expectations. "Well, Melinda, I would love nothing more than to believe your scenario, but there's also the possibility that the two of them are on a witch hunt, and their grief has taken the form of anger. We have to be prepared for anything."

Melinda had smiled at him, a smile of such warmth and innocence Percy had felt guilty for throwing such a wet blanket on the proceedings. "Very true Percy. But I've found that life is too short, and time is too fleeting to spend it expecting the worst." And that was that.

Now that the moment was nearly at hand, Beth was finding it more difficult to conjure up anything approaching Melindian confidence. She found herself fighting against a growing panic, a feeling of impending doom, that she was about to be thrown into the middle of a maelstrom of anger, grief, and accusation. She walked out on the deck and approached Percy, who was busy with the grill. "I have a bad feeling about all of this, but it's too late to back out now."

Percy put the tongs down and gave her a hug. "Yeah, I'm not feeling so great about this either, but I'm trying to channel my inner Melinda." Beth smiled and kissed him gently about the time that the doorbell rang.

It had been a 15-second eternity. Later Percy thought that if it were possible for time to stand still, it had when Beth had opened the door. There stood Christine and Christopher Harrison, aged 22, from Camden, Maine. As an only child, Percy had never known of brothers or sisters, and very little of kinship, or fraternity. Beth knew of it in theory only, as an abstract fact of biology. On this day she had opened her front door troubled by what these flesh and blood relations might have in store for her. She had not counted on the breathtaking intimacy that would come with a face-to-face introduction.

Everyone at the door had rehearsed the moment for weeks, but now there was just an airless silence, an electric flash of recognition that had sucked words out of the atmosphere before they could be heard. The only thing like it Percy had ever experienced was that magical quiet that would hush the plastic noise of a casino in that instant when Percy knew he had guessed right. Beth looked into their faces, first hers, then his. She raised her extended hand towards her lips in astonishment. The world slowed down as each of them took notice of the eyes, the curve and shape of the forehead, the line and length of the nose, the teeth, perfect and unnaturally white, the bow of the lips, and the gracefully curved lines of the chin. Percy heard the first word coming from Christopher, an epic understatement, "You must be Elizabeth Hope." The world resumed its ancient rhythm. The spell had been broken and the moment had passed.

Beth answered, "Yes, I am Beth Hope. You two must be Christopher and Christine then? Won't you come in?"

So much thought had been given to what would be said, and remain unsaid. Very little thought had been given to small talk. How does any conversation so fraught with uncomfortable possibility properly begin? Percy, seeing how rattled Beth had been at the door, rushed in to fill the gap. "I'm Percy, Beth's husband. How was the drive up from Richmond? I hope the traffic wasn't too difficult."

"No, it was pretty easy actually. Sorry, we're a bit early. We got here quicker than we intended." Christopher seemed to be the spokesman for the moment. "You have a beautiful home."

Jackets and sweaters were gathered. Everyone sat down in the living room. Beth seemed only interested in looking at them both, staring from one to the other and seeing herself staring back. Christopher began to warm to the task of keeping things moving. "We would like to thank you both for agreeing to see us and for your gracious invitation to dinner.

You didn't have to do either and we appreciate your cooperation and generosity."

Percy had noticed the word and secretly winced at its potential. "Cooperation" was something expected by law enforcement from witnesses to a crime. Christopher spoke with just a bit too much polish and practice, and Percy's guard went up. "Well, you guys came all the way from Maine, it was the least we could do. Speaking of dinner, I better go out to the grill and tend to it. I'll be just a minute." Percy hadn't wanted to leave them, but the meal needed some attention.

Beth noticed that the knuckles of Christine's hands were white from her tight grip. She looked about the room, at the paintings, the furniture, the rugs, anywhere but at Beth, while Christopher continued his free and easy monologue. "Virginia is a beautiful state. I actually thought about going to the University of Virginia, but decided against it, too far from home. I went to Dartmouth instead."

"Where did you go, Christine?" Beth asked, wanting desperately to hear her voice.

The question hung in the air, weak and crippled. Christine either hadn't heard, or was disinterested. Christopher stepped in with, "Christine?" His voice was loud and harsh.

Christine turned towards them as if startled. Her eyes seemed moist and frightened to Beth, and her hands remained locked in a vise grip of nervous tension. "I'm sorry. What was the question?" she managed to say.

"Mrs. Hope wanted to know where you went to college."

"Please, call me Beth. 'Mrs. Hope' makes me feel too old." Beth tried to lighten the mood.

"How old are you?" The question had shot out like a lasered accusation, impertinent and rude.

Christine sat up abruptly. "Chris! That's not a question you should ever ask a lady. Please excuse him. He must have picked up those bad manners at Dartmouth. I, on the other hand, had the good sense to attend the University of Maine."

"I went to Maryland. I'm a Terrapin, a 35-year-old Terrapin, I'm afraid."

Percy came through the door from the deck with a plate of perfectly grilled London broil and thought it best to pour the tea and set everything out on the table himself. When he finished, he entered the living room from the kitchen to gather everyone at the dinner table. The quiet that greeted him wasn't encouraging, but he screwed on his best Melinda smile and announced that dinner was served. Once they were all seated, Beth gathered herself and asked if she could offer a blessing. Percy couldn't believe his ears or his eyes as she reached out her hands to each side and took up his hand and Christine's. Suddenly, everyone was holding hands around the table, and Beth was smiling, bright and confident. Percy looked on in befuddled amazement as she closed her eyes and began, "Dear Father in heaven. Thank you for what we are about to receive. Thank you for safe travels for our friends. Bless our time together around this table. Amen." Percy opened his eyes, looked around the table, then at Beth, gave her hand a soft squeeze and said, "Amen."

◇ 23 ◇

Credibility

Percy had no appetite but was grateful to have food on his plate since it gave him something to pretend to be occupied with while trying to figure out what he could possibly have to say to the twins sitting across the table from him. Should he start the conversation or defer to Beth? Or, should he simply begin with some sort of nervous small talk about how unseasonably cool it had turned in the last few days? Perhaps the two of them had brought the cold with them from Maine? Maybe that would elicit a polite laugh, serve as an icebreaker.

Beth took a bite of the London broil and thought about complimenting the chef, but decided against it. It sounded too jolly, too familiar. Should she offer her condolences to them in a courteous attempt to bring up the subject of their 800-mile trip? Should she allow them to bring up the subject since, after all, this meeting was their idea? They were the ones who had asked for this. She decided to wait and say nothing.

Christine took a small bite of her food, terrified that everyone would notice that her hands were shaking. Now that she was here, in this house, sitting right beside her, she wanted to be anywhere else in the world but at this table. She had written the letter, she had sincerely wanted to meet with her, she needed to know. But she hadn't wanted to believe that she was her half-sister, but it was now undeniable. She was beautiful, she seemed nice, and she looked exactly like a sister was supposed to look... like her sister.

Christopher took a bite of the London broil, then a sip of tea. He then placed his utensils back at the sides of his plate, looked directly at Beth and began, "Mrs. Hope, my sister and I came all this way to find the answers to essentially two questions. The first answer was made plain to us the minute you opened your door. You are clearly our late father's daughter. The resemblance is uncanny and quite undeniable."

Percy had taken an instant dislike to Christopher earlier with his use of the word "cooperation," and now he was trying a bit too hard to sound more intelligent than he was. As a teacher of English literature at a school like UVA, he could spot guys like this from a mile away. Percy reminded himself to remain calm, but found himself saying, "And, what was the second question?"

Christopher kept his gaze squarely on Beth while replying, "The second question is, what exactly was the purpose of your visit? As far as we can tell, it was your first meeting with our father. You turn up in his office, and before the day is out, he commits suicide. Certainly you can understand why we might be curious."

"I'm sure that you are aware that the police asked us all about our meeting before we left Camden." Percy was growing more agitated by the minute.

"Yes. We read the reports. But it just didn't add up somehow. You had no contact with our father for practically all of your life, then randomly one day decided that you wanted to meet him, out of the blue, really, just a good old fashioned Thanksgiving meet and greet."

"Now, wait a minute!" Percy raised his voice and started to get up from the table when Beth reached out and held his hand. "Percy, it's ok. I'll be glad to answer your questions, Christopher. If I were in your shoes, I would feel the same way that you do." Beth looked at Christine, who had said nothing and looked on the edge of some sort of breakdown, ghostly pale with trembling hands, and eyes that pleaded for everything to be over. "When Percy and I left your father's office after our meeting, I had never been happier in my entire life. I had finally met my father, and it had gone well. I had left there thinking that I was beginning some sort of grand adventure. I was looking forward to years and years of building a relationship with him, of getting to know him. I even hoped to maybe one day meet you two. He showed me pictures of you guys. He was very proud of you both. So, when we woke the next morning and saw the police cars and heard the news, it came as a shock to both of us. But as shocked as I was, I can't imagine how horrible it must have been for you."

Christine had started to cry and Beth had reached out to hold her hand. Percy kept his eyes on Christopher, whose facial expressions had not changed as Beth had spoken. There was much of his father in his eyes, more energy, but the same suggestion of darkness. Suddenly, Christopher's voice changed, "Did I tell you how beautiful your house is? It's huge! Must be what, five, six bedrooms? Mind me asking how much a house like this costs in Virginia?"

"Excuse me?" Percy couldn't believe he had asked the question.

"Well, here's the thing." Christopher seemed to be enjoying himself. "Mr. Hope, you teach English at a community college and Mrs. Hope, you have a very spotty record of employment as a realtor. So, you can imagine how surprised Chrissy and I were when we pulled up in the driveway of this place. I had no idea that adjunct professors were so well paid."

Everything that Percy could think to say seemed like an escalation, so he decided to let the kid burn himself out. He reminded himself that Christopher was 22 years old and had just lost his father. He was hurting, and if Beth could stay calm, so could he.

"Now, Mrs. Hope, your speech was nice, really nice. But we're in a very difficult position here. The problem is, you guys just don't have a lot of credibility. I mean, I would like nothing better than to believe your story. Christine and I could just go on back to Maine satisfied that you had nothing whatsoever to do with our father's suicide. But why should I believe you when you've already lied to me once tonight? Mr. Hope, are you really Elizabeth's husband?"

Percy looked at Beth quickly, then back to Christopher, deciding not to answer. It wouldn't do much good to explain at this point anyway.

"I wasn't about to drive all this way without doing my homework. No, you two haven't been married for quite some time now. Matter of fact, Mrs. Hope, this beautiful house here, which somehow you two were able to pay cash for, was the crown jewel of your divorce settlement with Mr. Hope, isn't that right? Now, while I'm glad to see that you guys are getting along so well now, the fact is that you have quite a history, what with the divorce, some pretty God-awful gambling losses and a thankfully unsuccessful suicide attempt as well." The cocky grin that had been on Christopher's face disappeared as he leaned forward, placing his elbows on the table. "So please forgive me if I'm having a hard time buying your version of events."

Beth, still holding on to Percy's hand, gave him a quick glance, then turned to Christopher and stared at him in silence for what seemed to Percy to be an eternity. "Christopher, everything you just said is true, all of it."

From the very first minute he had walked into the house, Christopher had been a confident, self-assured young man on a mission. He felt he had arrived armed with the facts, and was determined to expose Beth and Percy as two reprobate grifters who had shown up at his father's office demanding money in exchange for their silence. He desperately wanted to believe that this blackmail attempt was the reason for his father's death, because the alternative, that Dillon Harrison's amoral lifestyle that had cost him his marriage had now driven him to suicide, was too painful to contemplate. Now, this woman wasn't even contesting his allegations. He had expected a fight or at least a more rigorous defense, but instead, here she was admitting that she was a lying goldbricker. Suddenly he was rattled.

"Percy and I got a divorce nearly five years ago now, and you're right, I did quite well in the settlement. You're also correct that Percy lost a lot of money gambling and he did try to kill himself, both because of me. The fact that we are getting along so well today is nothing short of a miracle, actually. Christopher, the truth is that I haven't lived a very good life. There are other sins that I'm guilty of that are even worse than the ones you listed. But there's one thing that I'm not guilty of: I didn't travel to Camden, Maine, to hurt your father. I wasn't there to confront him or scream at him for abandoning me when I was two years old. I was there because I needed to forgive him before I could begin to forgive myself for the mess I had made of my life. You don't have to believe me, and I wouldn't blame you if you didn't, but it's the truth."

Percy got up from the table in the silence and walked out of the room. Christine stopped crying long enough to ask Beth a question. "Did he know who you were?"

Beth was about to answer when Percy returned with Dillon's green metal lockbox and set it on the table in front of Christopher. "When we left Camden, Beth and I drove straight through the night, nearly 14 hours. When we pulled into the driveway, this box was on the front porch in an overnight package. Your father sent this from the UPS store right down the street from his office, and it was waiting for us when we got here. There was no note of explanation, no final words, nothing. If you can't bring yourself to believe us, maybe you can believe your own father."

Both of the twins recognized the green box. Both had walked in on their father many times at his office with this box opened on his desk. He would always scurry around, putting papers back inside and hustling it away, acting terribly busy, but thrilled to be interrupted. "Damned paperwork never stops!" he would say before giving them a big hug. And now, here it was sitting in front of them, filled with pictures of their half-sister, telling the story of her life. Christopher was finished talking.

◇ **24** ◇

Sleeping With One Eye Opened

In less than two weeks, Sam had gone from sleeping on a folded-up blanket under the awning of the deck to the ergonomic comfort of a memory-foamed doggie bed in the laundry room, to the library's loveseat. He had stormed into the hearts of his new owner and his girlfriend by means of a full-court charm offensive. This was no temperamental cat, judiciously dealing out its affections, carefully picking his spots. This was all in, unbridled adoration; the kind of delirious joy and boundless gratitude that only dogs rescued from hell have in such abundance. Although at first his kinetic energy and clumsiness seemed ill-suited for indoor living, Sam adjusted quickly, toned down the lamp-toppling tail wagging, and soon had the run of the place. Before stumbling through the forsythia bushes that night, Sam had spent his life observing humans mostly from a distance, carving out an existence on the edge between the wilderness and civilization. Now that he had a home, he simply couldn't bear being anywhere but in the shadow of his heroes.

Sam had fallen especially hard for Beth. Although Percy had been a pushover, Beth was at first less thrilled with his presence. As a consequence of her comparative coolness, Sam had singled her out for special affection. It had been a spectacular success. Beth delighted in the attention and tried to keep up by bringing him some new toy or treat practically every time she came over. It had been a match made in heaven.

But on this night, his owners weren't home. Sam was restless, pacing through the house, sniffing everything, looking for trouble. He had been disappointed when they didn't take him over to Beth's in the truck. He loved the truck, so high off the ground, the wind flapping his ears around. But this time they had left him at home, and he was having trouble settling down. He had eaten the food left for him and made a mess sloping water from his dish all over the laundry room floor, but that had been the only fun of the night. Now he was hearing every noise outside from miles around because Percy had left the sliding glass of the locked screen door open six inches at the bottom. When would they come home? Where were they? Why couldn't he come along? Sam flopped down on the matt in front of the refrigerator and let out a long sigh, and continued his all night vigil... waiting.

As the twins sifted through the photographs, Percy began taking the dishes away and busying himself in the kitchen. Beth sat with them, answering an occasional question from Christine. "Where was this one taken? How old were you in this one?" Christopher remained silent. His theory about Beth had blown up. Now he was faced with coming to terms with this beautiful woman across the table, who was growing more difficult to despise with every passing minute.

Christine pulled the newspaper clipping from the box, Beth's wedding photograph. "Wow, you were so beautiful. Not that you aren't still beautiful, but wow."

"That's very sweet of you to say. But it just occurred to me that I was about the same age as you when that picture was taken. If your hair were red instead of brown, that could be... you." Christine smiled shyly, and began to feel the mysterious stirrings of their connection, the power of blood. Beth looked at Christine once again, more carefully this time, less hurried and glancing a long direct gaze, and felt the same power, something close to love.

"I'll understand if neither of you want to talk about this, but what was he like?" Beth felt the risk was worth it. It might be her last chance to discover anything substantive about her father, what kind of man he was, and what kind of father, from the two people in the world who would know.

Christine put the pictures back in the box and looked down at her fingers, which became white with stress again. "He was a complicated man," she began. "I'm not sure where to begin."

"Well, you can start with the truth," Christopher suddenly interrupted. "Our father was a serial adulterer, a world class cheater. He spent half his life humiliating our mother until at last she finally had enough and divorced him."

"That's not the whole story," Christine shot back.

"It's close enough, and all Mrs. Hope here needs to know." Christopher backed his chair away from the table and looked as if he was ready to leave but remained seated.

Christine continued, only now looking up from her hand wringing full into Beth's eyes. "Dad loved us, and although it might sound strange, he loved Mom too. We were just never enough for him. It's not like he loved these women, it was mostly just one night stands, flings, really. But when he was home, he was very attentive to us, a good father."

Christopher, staring off into the distance, said to no one in particular, "That's like saying, 'Well, that Titanic sure was one hell of an impressive ship.'"

Christine was undeterred. "Dad had a great sense of humor. He was incredibly generous. He was probably the smartest man I've ever known. Chris has never forgiven him for hurting Mom, and I suppose, in truth, I haven't either. But I could never bring myself to hate him or disown him. I've been angry with him most of my life, still am on many levels." Tears began to form in her eyes, and Beth reached for a napkin and handed it to her. "But, he's still my father. You only get one father in this world, so you take the good with the bad. What else can you do?"

Sam was the sort of dog who, because of the hand he had been dealt, slept with one eye open. Even now that he lived in a real house with real, loving people, Sam was still a nervous sleeper. But on this night, for some reason, it was worse. His eyelids took turns turning upward; his ears would perk up at the slightest whisper of wind through the tops of the pines. Then he would drift off for a few minutes only to be stirred awake again by some troublesome snap or pop. Suddenly Sam felt especially uncomfortable, some sort of disturbance that caused the beginnings of a low growl to rise up from deep within him. He raised his head and tilted it to the side, straining to identify the noise. Slowly, he rose and skulked towards the screen door that led out to the deck. He pressed his flat, jet-black nose against the six-inch opening towards the bottom of the door, sniffing mightily. He looked out in every direction available to him. Nothing.

The conversation eventually came to a silent and uncomfortable end. No one had anything else to say. Percy had offered everyone coffee, but no one was interested. Finally, the twins made their way to the door. Christopher looked especially defeated, but managed to redeem his earlier rudeness by thanking Beth for agreeing to meet with them, and for being such a gracious host. Both of them thanked Percy for a great meal, even though much of it went uneaten. As they stood awkwardly in the doorway, Christopher shook Beth's hand and said, "After tonight, I think that Christine and I have to come to grips with the fact that our father killed himself because he was made miserable by the life that he lived, not because someone was trying to blackmail him. Deep inside I suppose I've known it all along. It's just hard to accept when the truth is so painful."

Beth took both of them by the hand. They looked startled, Percy even more so. Beth's voice began to tremble slightly, something Percy had never heard. "But what about us? My father died too. And now, you two amazing people walk into my house and I see myself in both of you. In a very miraculous way, we are a family. I'm not willing to walk away from that. I would love more than anything to get to know you, find out about your lives. I want the chance to love you like a brother and sister were meant to love each other. Would you let me do that? Can't we at least try?"

Christopher let go of Beth's hand. Christine lunged towards Beth, threw her arms around her and cried, "Yes! I would love that." Beth then turned towards Christopher. "What about you? Can we try to get to know one another?"

Christopher backed up a half a step, "Maybe."

Beth smiled, wiped the tears from her face and answered, "I'll take that. I'll take maybe."

Percy and Beth stood on the front steps and watched the tail lights of their rental car disappear. Then Beth collapsed into Percy's arms, overcome with exhaustion. "Let's go home."

"You are home."

"No, I meant your home. Can I stay with you tonight? We need to check on Sam anyway."

"Sure. Are you alright? That was a rough evening."

"I'm fine."

The low growl wouldn't stop coming as Sam paced from the screen door to the front door. There was no moon tonight, so dark out, he couldn't see the entire deck, the sliding swing beyond his field of vision. Something wasn't right. When would they come home? Strange smells from the back yard, moldy and acidic, something just beyond his view, Sam could feel it. No barking, because barking too much brings gunfire, can't bark, but nothing wrong with a few menacing growls. No more naps, must stand guard until they come home because something bad is out there, something smelly and desperate.

Beth threw some things in a bag. She hadn't spent the night at 16 Jennings Lane since that rapturous month a lifetime ago. They had not slept together since Maine. But for some inexplicable reason, Beth needed to feel safe. She needed to feel loved, and between Percy, Sam and that old house, she would. As she had sat listening to the twins talk about her father, feeling the warmth and kinship coming to life at the table, she realized that she could never leave Percy again. She loved him, and although she wasn't worthy of his love in return, she would have to accept it since somehow, against all odds and by the grace of God, he still loved her, and that was going to have to be enough. It had dawned on her in a flash as she had heard Christine say that you get only one father in life, so you must take the good with the bad. No plan of self improvement, no amount of penance, no regime of personal renewal would ever change the past. She would have to accept the freely granted forgiveness that Melinda talked about and start again with the only man who had ever loved her. She climbed into the truck, leaned over and kissed Percy. For the first time in her life, Beth Hope felt redeemed.

When the big truck pulled into the driveway, the motion-sensitive lights flared all around the exterior of the house illuminating the ground in yellow light. They both heard Sam's exasperated barks from the inside of the house. This was a new and odd sound; neither Beth nor Percy could ever recall ever hearing Sam bark before. "He probably just really has to pee," Percy offered as explanation. "Poor boy."

Percy unlocked the side door from the carport that entered into the laundry room, saw the water on the floor and braced for Sam's always manic welcome home dance to begin; only Sam didn't come. He was standing at the screen door at the far end of the kitchen, barking and growling menacingly, then glancing back over his shoulder at the two of them.

"What's the matter, Sam?" Beth was the first to reach him. "You need to go outside?" She unlatched the door and Sam bolted through, slamming the door open hard against the side of the house.

"What the hell?" Percy held Beth back from the deck, stepped in front of her and followed Sam outside. Sam was in a panic, racing from one end of the yard to the other, stopping only to sniff the ground. The hair on his back was raised to a coiled point from his collar to his tail, and he wouldn't stop growling.

"There's nothing out here, boy. It's alright, calm down Sam." After several minutes, Sam reluctantly gave up the search, jumped back on the deck and through the kitchen door, then noticed Beth for the first time. The dance finally began.

◆ **25** ◆

Super 8

Her hair was dirty and pulled back tightly into a ponytail, streaks of grey running in greasy crooked lines. Her face was creased with long, deep wrinkles across her forehead and crow's feet around her eyes. She had the look of someone who had spent a lot of time braving the elements, working outside in the sun, except that she was skin and bones, a body too frail to ever have been capable of hard labor. Still, her face had about it the possibility of beauty, the suggestion that perhaps in an earlier time she may have been pretty. Her hands were dirty and shaking as she struggled to light a cigarette. Her duffle bag was at her feet as she stood shaking in the cold night air, hidden behind the huge cover of forsythia bushes. Her mind raced. She hadn't counted on Percy Hope having company. She had hoped to catch him alone, but not only did he apparently have a girlfriend, but a dog too, so many complications! But she had come a long way, and there could be no turning back. There was nowhere else to go.

Beth had played with Sam for a while, then gotten ready for bed. She was surprised to discover that Percy's bedroom was the old junk room, the smallest in the house. "Why did you put your bed in here? It hardly fits. This has got to be the smallest bedroom I've ever seen!"

"It's complicated." Percy was embarrassed. "It felt weird to sleep in their old room, and my old bedroom didn't seem right either, so I ended up back here."

Beth stood in the doorway, leaning against the inside of the frame smiling at Percy, looking amazing. "Well. I suppose it will have to do..."

"Oh, I'm sorry. I just assumed you would take my old room," Percy teased.

"Not a chance, sailor. Scoot over."

Afterwards, they lay in each other's arms and drifted off to sleep, Sam keeping an anxious vigil on the mat in front of the refrigerator, one eye open.

Beth stirred in the night, an unfamiliar sound. Now awake, her eyes began to adjust to the darkness. Lying next to him, she felt safe. She pulled the covers up tighter around her neck and edged closer to him, but Percy was out cold. A warm smile spread over her face in the darkness. Finally, she was happy.

She heard the raspy, hoarse caw of the raven down the hall. Four AM. The clock never failed to surprise her. Now she was wide awake. She got up to get some water and pat Sam's head, but he wasn't in the kitchen; must have decided to sleep in his bed in the laundry room. She opened the door to the refrigerator and found virtually nothing, so typical of Percy. When she closed the door, all the air rushed from her lungs. She tried to scream but no sound came. There, sitting at the kitchen table, was an old trash heap of a woman with dark, hollow eyes, covered in wrinkles and smelling old and sick. Beth wanted to scream for help but couldn't. Where in God's name was Sam? How did this woman get into the house?

"Not exactly the sort of hospitable reception I was hoping for, but I can't really say that I blame you. You don't even know who I am, do you?"

Her voice was ancient and fragile, but not threatening. The

sound of it worked its way through the mist of the moment and delivered a hint, an invitation of sorts. Beth blinked back the tears of terror in her eyes and strained to take a closer look. A beam of light flashed off the screen door, the rapid click-click-click of an old Super 8 movie. There she was, flowing red hair, provocative sweater, heavy make-up and a radiant smile. Her mouth was moving, forming words without sound. She was beaming with pride in the bright sunshine, holding a baby in a frilly white dress, looking for all the world to see, like a movie star. Then a handsome young man in a dark suit and slicked back hair appeared on the screen, looking somewhat embarrassed, as if he would rather be anywhere else in the universe than posing for family movies with the bubbly, energetic beauty beside him. It was Dillon looking so tortured, standing next to the voluptuous Jill Chester. The movie ended as if the celluloid had been set ablaze. The light went dark and the old woman spoke again, "Elizabeth. It's me. It's your mother."

Beth turned in panic and ran down the hall as fast as her legs would carry her, giant swift strides, athletic and graceful. In the distance she heard Percy calling to her. He was on his way. She could see him now at the other end of the hall, arms extended, calling her name, "Beth! It's alright, Beth!!"

She awoke with a start and gasped for breath like she had been underwater too long. She looked at Percy's face and heard his voice telling her that he was here, everything was alright, and it had all been a dream.

Beth sat on the loveseat, her knees pulled tightly to her chest. Percy had picked up some bagels for breakfast and was trying to change the subject from the dream, without success.

"It seemed so real. I'm not sure I'll ever get that face out of my mind."

"It may have seemed real, Beth, but there's no way in hell Sam would have let anyone in this house."

"I know, I know."

"You had just had a very trying and traumatic day spent thinking about your dad, your past. It was only natural that you might have a dream about your mother."

This was the thing about Percy that Beth needed in her life, his emotionless, analytical detachment. He had the rare ability in a crisis to break down an emotionally charged event into its underlying component parts without sounding like a bloodless bureaucrat. Percy was no Spock; he cared deeply, and was fully committed to her, but was able to inject rational thought into a charged moment, placing all the fire and fury into calm perspective. "Besides," he continued, "there's something about this old house that encourages vivid dreams. You used to appear to me sitting in that very love seat so real I could smell your perfume. It wouldn't surprise me if one day a tribe of Indians show up on my front yard demanding that I tear the place down because it was built over the top of graves of their ancestors."

Beth threw her napkin at him. "Thanks for putting that lovely mental image in my head!"

"Well, at least it stopped you from thinking about your mom! I've spent enough time in therapy to pick up a few tricks of the trade."

They spent the remainder of the morning eating bagels and playing with Sam, enjoying how easy it had suddenly become to think and act like a couple. When they were married everything seemed like a battle of wills, a competition for control. With the divorce came a vengeful bitterness. Now, they had found an easy freedom together, as if they had just met and become smitten again, a miraculous journey that neither of them could quite believe. In this chapter of their lives together, it was Percy who asked the question, and within 30 minutes, they found themselves knocking on Dave and Melinda's apartment door at 10:30 in the evening.

Dave seemed surprised to see them; Melinda's smile wasn't as luminous as usual, but in their defense, it was late, and they hadn't called to give them any warning. Percy felt suddenly silly for being so impetuous, "Guys, I'm awfully sorry for showing up like this without calling first."

"No, no. Come in, come in. What in the world brings you two all the way out here at this hour?"

Beth gave Melinda a hug and noticed that she didn't look well and wasn't as giddily happy to see her as she usually was. She was six months pregnant, Beth reminded herself; the poor thing was probably exhausted. Then she saw the wadded clumps of used tissues on the end table, noticed suddenly that the television wasn't on, and that her eyes were puffy. "Melinda, what's wrong?"

Percy had been about to blurt out his intention to remarry Beth, that they didn't feel right living together, that they wanted to make things right again between them and that they wanted Dave to do the honors, nothing fancy, just a small private affair between them and God, when he heard the concern in Beth's voice, and noticed the stillness in the room, the heaviness of the silence. Melinda sat down slowly on the sofa and spoke the feeble words barely above a whisper, "There's something wrong with the baby."

Beth dropped to her knees beside her and held her hand, listening to the news. They had gone for a checkup earlier, just a routine 24-week visit, and the doctor had found something that had made him leave the room with his nurse and return a minute later with another doctor. Soon the room had been crowded with smiling nurses telling her everything was fine even though Melinda knew that everything was definitely not fine. Finally the doctor had told them that the baby had a heart problem, something that had never been detected up until now, some sort of defect that was serious enough for them to suggest the possibility of open fetal surgery. Beth began to cry, and Percy put his arm around Dave.

"At this point we're just trying to adjust to the news," Melinda continued. "It's not the sort of news anyone wants to hear, but Dave and I have no choice but to trust God and know that he will never allow us to endure something without first empowering us with what we need to overcome. I don't cry for me, I cry for my child. I cry because I wish it were me and not him."

Her words were delicate and hung in the air, forlorn and unanswerable. Eventually the mood lightened, and the conversation shifted to the purpose of their visit. Percy made something up about having been in the neighborhood and just wanting to check in to see how they were doing. Nobody believed it, but nobody had been in the mood to prolong the uncomfortable intrusion into such a painful and private moment that Percy's ill-timed spontaneity had become. Goodbyes were said, promises to call tomorrow were offered, and then Percy had driven back to 16 Jennings Lane listening to Beth crying, the second time in six months he had witnessed her sobbing like a child, broken down and inconsolable. Once home, Beth had changed into some pajamas and curled up on the loveseat in the library. Percy thought it best to give her some space, but Sam was having none of it. He walked into the library, jumped up on the loveseat beside Beth, and laid his head down on her feet. Beth patted his head. "Oh, Sam, you're such a good boy."

◇ **26** ◇

Caritas

The shiny red plastic plate was covered with baked beans, swimming in dark sauce with a curled strip of bacon laced throughout. A square piece of cornbread sat propped up on the edge of the plate, its lower half soaking up the juice from the beans. A ham sandwich on rye bread with mayonnaise and a slice of American cheese sat alone, separated from the beans by a raised divider that ran down the middle of the plate. There was a serving of canned peaches in a small plastic bowl. Someone had drained all the thick syrup from them, so they just sat there looking dry and hard. There was a paper napkin on the table to her right and a glass of iced tea with a fat slice of lemon balanced on the rim. In the middle of the table was a basket with piles of jams and jellies in little sealed containers, strawberry, grape and peach. On the napkin was a plastic knife, fork and spoon.

The place looked like a typical downtown homeless shelter, but it had turned out to be a church, one of the new kinds with no steeple, and no old people, where no one wore suits. They must have bought some old broken down warehouse and fixed it up, but not too well since it still looked like an old warehouse. There was a big banner hanging across one of the walls with huge happy letters... "Community Feast Night," it said. But from the looks of the 50 or so souls greedily devouring their food, it looked more like your basic garden variety "feed the derelicts night." But she didn't care. She was hungry.

As she ate she glanced around at the bright, shining faces of the ladies in their white aprons, smiling at everyone and everything as if serving dinner to 50 of life's biggest losers, wreaking of urine and vomit, was just about the greatest thing imaginable. The men were even more astounding in their enthusiasm, especially the good-looking one who was making the rounds from table to table, chatting up everyone who would listen. She heard his young, unknowing voice talking about the love of God. "Easy for him to say," she thought, "he's wearing a bright shiny wedding ring, clean clothes and he doesn't smell like shit." As he cleared the corner of her table and started heading her way, she lowered her head and got busy with her beans, trying not to be noticed.

"Hello there. I'm not sure I've seen you here before. This is your first visit?"

She kept her head down and made no reply, hoping he would move along to the next table. His voice was energetic and inviting, yet still flowed with the languid peacefulness of the South.

"Well, sure am glad you came, dear. If you need anything just let me know. My name's Dave. What's yours?"

More beans, then a bite of the cornbread, and he was gone.

"Where's Dave?" Beth asked as soon as she walked through the apartment door. Ever since she had heard the news about the baby, she had attended to Melinda's every need. This morning, it was bringing her a breakfast of bacon, egg, and cheese biscuits from Hardees.

"He's over at church. We're doing that Caritas thing this week, remember?"

"Oh, yeah!" Beth had forgotten all about the homeless

thing that Dave had signed the church up for, and was a bit annoyed that Dave hadn't gotten someone else to take his spot for the overnight shift, considering what his wife was going through at home. But, that wasn't Dave's way, or Melinda's really. So, here she was, alone in her tiny apartment while her husband was up all night feeding a church full of homeless people.

"He called this morning and said they had 47 people show up for dinner and stay the night. He sounded exhausted but thrilled at the same time for the opportunity to love those poor people."

"I would have preferred that he were here, loving you." Melinda couldn't hide her disappointment. "Any news from the doctor?"

Melinda tore into the biscuit, the most powerful craving of her pregnancy, then took a sip of orange juice. "Yes. They've decided not to do the fetal surgery. They will instead monitor me very closely over the next few weeks and try for a normal delivery and then do the operation after the birth. There is risk in waiting, but some advantages too, so Dave and I are trusting the doctors and trusting God. That's all we can do at this point."

Melinda had good days and bad. This was a good day. Her eyes were brighter, her mood more optimistic. After devouring the biscuit, she laughed. "Good Lord, I would give a million bucks for a cup of coffee right now!"

Beth laughed along with her, continually amazed at the resilience of her friend. Ever since learning about the baby's heart trouble, Beth had carried with her a secret fear, a shameful thought. Melinda resided at the top of a holy pedestal in Beth's mind. She was an angel in human form, proof that it was possible to be genuinely good. Melinda's faith wasn't some mindless dogma that turned her into something perfect and unapproachable, but at the same time, her faith did make her special, a living example of what an authentic Christian might look like. Now, with the terrible news about her unborn child, so unfair and undeserved, Beth feared that Melinda would lose her faith, become angry at God for his betrayal. Would she fall from her pedestal, crash to the ground in a broken heap with the rest of humanity, and become filled with anger and bitterness? Was it ridiculously unfair for Beth to have placed her on such a pedestal in the first place? Probably, but knowing someone good enough to be in that place had saved Beth's life.

But, as Beth observed her every day, she saw the tears, she saw the fear, but Melinda's faith had never wavered. She had managed to maintain her blissful confidence. She still viewed her world as a place of grand possibility, each day as an opportunity to "be a blessing to someone." Beth thought it was a fascinating way to live as she watched Melinda tear into her second biscuit.

"When I'm done, let's head over to church and help out Dave for a bit. Okay?" It was the last thing in the world Beth wanted to do. Having grown up poor and homeless half the time, she had no desire to be reminded of what it was like all over again, but she could hardly say no to her friend.

"Sure, if that's what you'd like."

Jill Chester chose the cot in the far corner. She wanted to be as far away from everyone else as possible, and the fact that her corner was close to the bathroom didn't hurt. The pains in her abdomen were getting sharper and more frequent. The waves of nausea came less often than they used to, but when they did, she needed to be close to a toilet. It was a miserable existence that was only going to get worse. She was running out of time. It was the reason she had taken the midnight bus ride that had taken so much out of her in the first place. Her variety of pancreatic cancer was the fatal kind. It was now or never.

After the meal was served, a group of impossibly happy kids cleaned up the mess. Then, several men folded up the metal tables and wheeled them out of sight. The cots were placed in neat rows, each of them made up with clean sheets and blankets. After everyone got settled, Jill winced when she saw the guitars coming out of their cases, the cables and cords being unwound, and the microphone stands being put in place. She always hated this part. They just fed you and provided you with a safe place to sleep for the night, so it was the least she could do to listen to the music, her debt of gratitude. But she still hated every minute of it. It brought back memories of Dillon and the hateful rejection of his church, the one she had been forced to attend for two years, the one where she first learned what a filthy, miserable sinner she was. But that was an eternity ago. Now, she would lie on her cot obediently and listen to the pretty blonde girl sing Amazing Grace, not believing a word of it.

Sometime around midnight, she hurried to the bathroom and threw up. It had come upon her quickly, and she was glad to have chosen a cot so close. Afterwards, she had splashed cold water on her face and immediately felt better. Back in her cot she had quickly fallen asleep, when she felt the soft, moist tongue of a dog licking her hand. She looked down and saw him, a beautiful yellow lab lying at her feet, eyes closed, licking every inch of her hand. It was as if he knew that she was ill, that she had cancer, and he was trying to clean it off of her hand. He looked up at her, seemed to smile, and she acknowledged his efforts with a pat of the head. He returned to his work as the beautiful woman walked into the kitchen and opened the refrigerator door. She jumped at the sight of her, eyes wide with panic. There was a flash of light. They recognized each other, then another flash of light, and an old mechanical sound, a buzzing hum and a soft click, click, click. There they were, young and beautiful, in the sparkling spring sunshine, her red hair, her baby girl in that frilly white dress. She looked up at the beautiful woman and managed a weak smile. "Elizabeth. It's me. It's your mother."

It was the same dream she had had almost every night since her diagnosis. The first night it had been a nightmare and she had woken up sweating and terrified. Then, after a while, the dream brought with it only regret and longing. But now, after four months, it had become something sweet, a fleeting but magical glimpse into the face of her grown daughter. The only thing keeping her alive was the mission to find her, to find the daughter of her dreams.

◊ **27** ◊

"Elizabeth?"

Percy and Sam had become inseparable, so when Dave had asked him to consider helping out with Caritas Week, Percy had said, "Only if I can bring Sam." Dave had thought it a great idea, thinking that seeing a friendly dog might go a long way towards lifting everyone's spirits. So, Sam had jumped up onto the passenger seat of the truck and rode to church after dinner. Percy had volunteered to be in charge of moving tables and setting up the cots after the evening meal.

Percy hadn't been prepared for the smell of 50 homeless people, the pungent stench of body odor and the overpowering aroma of humidity and dirty clothes. These were people who spent all of their lives outdoors, and they brought the smell of raw humanity inside with them, setting them apart from the rest of mankind, those lucky enough to live inside. Percy stayed busy with the thousand things that needed to be done to properly care for so many hungry people, but between jobs he watched Dave walking from one of them to the next, smiling and topping off their glasses with tea. Dave made it a point to touch each of them, a pat on the back, or a handshake, a tacit acknowledgement that he cared for them and wasn't put off by their filth. Some of them seemed pleased with the attention and smiled at him, engaging in conversation, but most ignored him altogether.

None of them ignored Sam, who quickly became the center of attention. His huge tail wagging, Sam would walk up to each of them and stick his nose under their arm, hoping for a scratch or a treat. Percy marveled at the transformation that would come over their faces. When moments before they looked beaten and angry, their faces twisted and gnarled by exposure and bad luck, suddenly their features would soften at the sight of Sam, smiles appearing out of nowhere, suggesting that somewhere, a long time ago, they might have been happy.

Percy helped set up the makeshift stage for the college kids who would be singing some songs for the crowd. Then he lined up the metal folding chairs in neat rows. Almost everyone made their way over, took a seat and listened politely. Dave and Percy stood in the back feeling exhausted. Their shift was just beginning. For security purposes, several men were needed to stay the night just in case there was trouble. In a crowd this size, the chances that someone might get violent had to be considered. Percy tapped Dave on the arm and pointed over into the far corner. "Looks like Sam has made a friend."

There he was sitting beside Jill on her cot. She was patting his head and talking to him, a broad smile on her face. Sam's tail was thumping hard against her pillow.

"Oh. That's the lady who wouldn't give us her name, would only give us her initials... JC. She wouldn't give me the time of day. Sure glad you brought Sam."

As the pretty blonde singer began a sweet acoustic guitar version of Amazing Grace, Percy saw JC gaze off into the distance while Sam began feverishly licking her hands. Her thoughts seemed so far away, and her expression darkened. Still, Sam kept licking, carefully, methodically, every inch of one hand, then the other. Percy's first thought had been one of disgust. Where, in God's name, had those hands been? But then it all became something very different, something kind and sweet. She looked at Sam with benign confusion, watched his soft pink tongue cleaning her hands with such tenderness, and wondered why. Percy listened to the words of the song, "*Through many dangers, toils and snares I have already come.*" He looked at JC, now curled up next to Sam on the cot, and wondered how long it had been since anyone had paid as much attention to her as Sam had over the past 30 minutes. When morning came, Sam was still on the floor next to Jill's cot, as if he were on vigil, still licking her hand that hung over the side near his head. It was the oddest thing, Percy thought. Even when the men began stirring, making noise setting up the tables for breakfast, Sam stayed at Jill's side.

Jill felt warm air against her face, opened her eyes and was instantly wide awake. The dog was still there, his glistening black nose six inches from her, his huge pink tongue flopping in and out of his smiling mouth. Jill smiled and reached out to him, scratching the close blond fur between his eyes. "Are you still here? You need to pay attention to somebody else or they are gonna get jealous."

It felt strange to hear herself speak at all, but especially words so full of sweetness, so light and full of care. Jill had been silenced by her life, had lost the desire to speak, to be heard. All of the hard living, the drugs, the exhausting nomadic existence had taken words from her. She had learned that talking too much could get her into trouble. Nobody needed to know what she was thinking, and nobody cared anyway, so she had retreated into a world of silence, sometimes going weeks at a time without speaking a word. But now she found herself looking into the warm, inviting eyes of a dog and saying, "I wish I knew your name, boy. You sure are a sweet one."

"His name is Sam, and he seems to have fallen for you." Percy smiled.

Jill hadn't noticed him standing there, hadn't noticed anything but the dog. She kept her eyes on Sam, kept scratching his head and refused to look up.

Suddenly Jill realized that she was extraordinarily hungry, such an odd sensation. Since the cancer, she was never hungry, only ate out of instinct, and never thought about food. Now, she smelled bacon cooking off in the distance, heard the laughter of women and the cling-clang of pots and pans from the kitchen, and would have given anything for a stack of buttermilk pancakes with maple syrup.

"Breakfast will be ready in a few minutes. Are you hungry?"

Jill looked up at Percy, studied his face for a moment, recognized it from the picture she had cut out of the newspaper and carried with her the picture of him in his tuxedo and Elizabeth in her fine dress. He was older but it was him, no doubt about it. "Yes. I actually am hungry this morning." They were the first words she had spoken to another human being in months.

Percy watched a group of middle school boys in little league uniforms carrying plates of scrambled eggs, bacon and toast from the kitchen out to the long tables. He watched them set the plates in front of men and women ranging in age from 28 to 68, about half of them black and half white. JC sat alone at the end seat of an empty table, Sam still by her side. Percy noticed that she looked up at the red-haired boy in the Orioles uniform, smiled at him and mouthed the words, "Thank you." Dave made his way between the tables with a pot of coffee, stopping to chat with anyone who gave him the slightest opening. When he reached JC, she looked up at him for the first time.

"Looks like you've made a friend."

JC nodded her head and managed a smile. Then she looked at the thick white coffee mug turned upside down in front of her. She reached out and turned it over. Dave poured it full. "Don't let Sam sucker you out of that bacon."

Dave turned to leave and was startled to hear her voice. "Sam here belongs to that man over there by the trash can. Do you know him?"

"I sure do. That's Percy Hope."

"Is he married?"

"Why? Are you interested?" It was one of the things about his personality that annoyed him, his tendency towards awkward attempts at humor at extraordinarily unfunny moments. This particular attempt embarrassed JC, and as soon as he said it, he knew that he had lost her. He attempted to recover with, "Actually, Percy is not married, but he has a girlfriend who oddly enough used to be his wife, but now they are just dating." The more he talked, the worse it got, until finally he left her to her breakfast and scurried back to the kitchen feeling like an insensitive brute.

The eggs tasted better than anything she had eaten in years. To her amazement, she found herself spreading orange marmalade over her toast, savoring every bite. The bacon was smokey and crisp, a little burnt around the edges like she liked. She poured some milk into her coffee, turning it the color of caramel, and it was smoother than anything she could remember drinking in the longest time. Such an odd feeling had come over her, something soothing and unfathomable. She looked down at Sam; saw his dark, wet eyes looking up at her and felt a strange comfort. She knew she was very close to finding her child, and she knew she was dying, and yet, here in a drafty warehouse in Virginia, the permanent knot in her stomach had at long last loosened its grip. "Thank you, Sam."

Beth drove into the parking lot, turned off the engine, and took a deep breath. Melinda reached across and held her hand. "Listen, I know you're nervous about this, but you need to trust me. You have no idea how much of a blessing this is going to be. Every time I have ever worked a Caritas event, I've come away feeling like I've actually made a difference. It's a wonderful feeling... relax."

It occurred to Beth that Melinda was the type of woman who would walk into the middle of an Al Qaeda planning meeting in downtown Islamabad if there was even the most remote chance to "be a blessing" to someone, so her little speech did little to take away the pit in her stomach. But if she was ever going to walk into another homeless shelter, it would only be with Melinda at her side. "Ok, ok! I'll go in with you. But it doesn't mean I have to be thrilled about it, and there's no guarantee I won't leave after five minutes."

"Absolutely," Melinda agreed with a huge smile on her face, "but after you've had the most amazing morning of your life, I'm going to say I told you so!"

They entered the building from the back where Dave's office was located, across the hall from the kitchen, which was a beehive of activity, ladies laughing, the sound of bacon frying, and the smell of strong coffee. Beth was relieved to see Percy walk through the swinging doors that led into the old warehouse. He was carrying a huge plastic bag full of garbage out to the dumpster, when he spotted her. "Well, hello beautiful. I didn't expect to see you. Did Melinda drag you here kicking and screaming?"

"Kicking and screaming, but she's here," Melinda answered.

Somehow, knowing that Percy was there made things better. He was good that way. "What are you doing here?" Beth asked.

"Dave pestered me about this to the point where I had to say yes to shut him up. But from the look of things, what he really wanted was Sam."

"You brought Sam here?"

"You should see that dog. He's the star of the show, and he's made a special friend. There's a woman out there who he attached himself to last night, and he hasn't left her side ever since. Go look!"

Beth walked hesitantly through the swinging doors as if they were a portal into the labyrinth of her tortured childhood. The first third of her life had been a string of loud, smelly rooms just like this one, filled with collections of damaged people, all the product of bad decisions, bad luck or worse, just plain evil. Her mother had been a combination of all three. But here, now, walking through the doors and seeing them, all so unchanged and eternal, she felt ten again. The smells were the same, the slouched shoulders, the filthy clothes. Beth felt tears forming in her eyes, knowing that it had been a terrible decision to come here, to dredge it all up again. She would find Sam and take him home. This Good Samaritan thing was for people like Melinda and Dave, and even Percy, people who weren't raised by a drug-addicted prostitute.

She saw Sam over in the far corner by a cot, sitting at the feet of an old lady with a long ponytail. Beth cupped her hands around her mouth and hollered, "Sam!" Sam and the old woman turned to face her. Sam barked and wagged his tail frantically but wouldn't leave her side. Beth made her way around the rows of tables over to the cots. Sam barked again, obviously thrilled to see her, even reared up on his hind legs in excitement. Beth smiled at Sam's playfulness and realized how much she had grown to love him in just a few short months. She reached out and gave him a hug and scratched him vigorously on his head.

"Sorry if Sam here has been bothering you, but I've got to take him home now," Beth said without looking up.

"Elizabeth?" Jill's voice had aged, was quieter, less angry, but it resonated through the years with the ring of clarity, a muted scream through a bullhorn, a sound dripping with memory. Beth stood up slowly and faced her, looked into her wrinkled face, smelled the breath reeking of cigarettes and vomit, and saw the green eyes filling with tears.

"Mom?"

$$\diamond\ \textbf{28}\ \diamond$$

"A beautiful lie beautifully told"

Percy and Beth had taken her home, back to 16 Jennings Lane. Few words were spoken. Melinda had gone by Walmart to get her some new clothes. Beth had insisted that she take a shower when they arrived at the house. Sam laid at the bathroom door in the hallway until she was finished. Melinda gave them all hugs and then left the three of them alone at the kitchen table. Jill was still hungry and asked for a sandwich. Percy sat a plate in front of her with a peanut butter and jelly sandwich and some Doritos.

"How did you find me?" Beth asked.

"Wasn't hard," Jill answered between bites. "With Google now, it's pretty hard to disappear."

Beth looked at her mother across the table devouring the sandwich. She looked about as she imagined she might after all this time. The biggest surprise of the day hadn't been that her mother had appeared out of nowhere after 15 years; the biggest surprise was that she was alive at all. On the rare occasions when Beth had allowed herself to think of her mother, it had been to wonder how she had died. Had she gotten AIDS or been murdered in some alley somewhere? But here she was, looking old and beaten up by life, but still alive, a survivor.

"Why now?" Beth asked.

"Because I'm dying. I have cancer and I don't have very long, they tell me. I figured that if I was ever going to see you again I better get busy." Beth said nothing, just stared back at her in silence. "Besides, nobody wants to die alone, even someone like me."

"Someone like you?" Beth felt the stirrings of some very old anger.

"Yeah, someone like me. I'm a terrible person, Elizabeth, I know. You don't owe me a goddamned thing. But when you're about to die, you have nothing to lose. Maybe you can do one decent thing in your life, maybe you can try to make things right, although it's impossible, you still feel like trying and maybe if there's just one thing on the scales in my favor at the end, it would be better than nothing."

Jill finished her sandwich, gobbled up the chips and began patting Sam's head, still at her side, something that was starting to annoy Beth.

"What kind of cancer?" Beth's questions were short and sharp.

"Pancreatic."

"Do you have any proof?"

"Proof? You mean like from a doctor?"

"Yes, from a doctor. You show up here after 15 years of nothing with a story about cancer, and you expect me to take your word for it?" Percy grimaced and picked up the plate from in front of Jill and began washing it in the sink, eager for an excuse to escape the increasingly tense encounter.

"Well, I travel kinda light. I don't have my medical records with me."

"Then, we'll take you to our doctor tomorrow."

"Tomorrow? I didn't even know there would be a tomorrow."

"If you're sick, I'm not going to throw you out on the street. I owe you that much. Can she stay here tonight, Percy?"

Percy dried his hands with the dish towel. "Sure. It's a little crowded, but we can make it work. We might be more comfortable over at your place."

"No. I'll feel more comfortable here."

Having a plan for the next 24 hours calmed everyone's nerves. Jill seemed grateful just to be there. Beth tried to ignore her as much as she could. Percy couldn't keep his eyes off Sam, who still seemed enamored with Jill and wouldn't leave her side. After dinner, they all gathered out on the deck. It was a beautiful night with a soft breeze stirring through the top of the pines. Sam showed no interest in playing catch. Beth tried to look interested in the book in her hands while Jill seemed overcome with the beauty of the back yard, its yellow flowers, the finely trimmed lawn, the exquisite privacy of it all. "... and you guys can sit out here every night if you want to, I bet."

Percy smiled. "Well, at least until summer comes. Then it's too danged hot."

"Not tonight though, it's beautiful out." Jill felt a wave of gratitude come over her. She didn't deserve this, to be taken in this way. Beth had every right to throw her out on the street. As she took a deep breath and caught a whiff of honeysuckle, it occurred to her that she hadn't thrown up all day, since the previous night at the shelter.

After a while, Beth went back inside, and for the first time, Sam went with her, leaving Jill and Percy on the deck. The breeze had died down. Soon the crickets would start to sing, but for now, the two of them sat alone in the heavy silence. Percy could see through the years on Jill's face, and despite the lines and creases, there was evidence of Beth. He wanted to know the story, but he didn't have the nerve to ask.

"The man back at the church told me that you two used to be married but that now you're just dating. How's that working?"

Percy couldn't help smiling. "Well, it's a very long story."

"Well, since I'm dying, if you're gonna tell me, you better get started."

Beth stood at the kitchen door and listened to Percy's version of their life story. She listened to the soft words, the tender phrases. Percy's story had washed away all of her failures. To hear him tell it, Beth had saved his life. There was no mention of her shallowness, her selfishness or her infidelity. It was a beautiful love story, a story of redemption in which she played the lead role. It was the type of story that gets made into a movie, where patience and love triumph over all enemies. It was a beautiful lie beautifully told by a man who wanted to give a dying mother someone to be proud of.

Jill listened without saying a word, content to hear it in its entirety, like a freshly written poem. When Percy had exhausted himself, they noticed that the crickets had begun to sing somewhere during the telling. The sound had a pulsing quality, a soothing steadiness that filled the void left by Percy's silence.

Jill stared past the pine trees into the stars. "It's a miracle she turned out so well. I gave her nothing, you know. Anything good in her came from God or her father, and I doubt anything good could have come from him, so I suppose it must have been God."

It was the only thing she said the rest of the night. Percy made a bed for her in his old bedroom. When he said goodnight and shut the door, Sam walked over from his bed in the utility room and curled himself into a tight ball at her door.

After midnight, the grass was heavy with dew. It felt good on her bare feet. The moon was up, lighting the back yard in patches here and there where its beams managed to drift through the pines. In the back corner, at the property line, was one such place, at the edge of the forsythia bushes. From a distance there appeared to be a silver plate on the ground. She walked towards it and it changed from silver to dark grey, from shiny to dull the closer she got. As she stood directly over the spot, she saw the round grey stone, with words carved on the surface; beautiful flowing script like an expert calligrapher might write them with long elegant strokes, lovely and dramatic. "We Love You, Dear Sam."

"What an odd thing to say," she thought, "and what an odd place to put such a stone, way in the back corner of the yard where no one can see it." Still, it was a beautiful backyard, and she could hardly think of a nicer place to walk if you couldn't get to sleep.

She returned to the deck and sat down in the sliding swing, gliding back and forth. She noticed that although the thing looked old, it didn't squeak. Percy took care of things, looked after his property, which spoke well of him. There wasn't a blade of grass out of place anywhere on the place, and you couldn't say that about very many people anymore.

She was startled when the kitchen door opened. Beth had a robe on over her pajamas and didn't seem surprised to see her mother outside at one o'clock in the morning. She walked past her to the stairs that led down to the yard and sat with her back to her on the top step, never acknowledging her presence. Jill rocked back and forth, searching for words. "Sorry to see I'm not the only one who can't sleep," was what she came up with, and Beth hadn't responded. But that was alright with Jill, since Beth didn't owe her anything.

Minutes passed, and the silence became comforting. Here they were, after all this time, sitting together under the stars, not arguing, just together. Jill began to feel the strange new peace that had been surprising her ever since she had been awakened by Sam's breath early that morning. She felt alive and optimistic about things in a way that defied logic, given her prognosis. And yet, here she was listening to herself say, "Percy and I had a long talk earlier. He told me the story about you two. It was a beautiful story. I told him what I'm going to tell you now, the fact that you turned out so well was no thanks to me. I couldn't be more proud of you, Elizabeth. You've found yourself a wonderful man, and he adores you, which is about all any woman can ask for. Good for you, child."

Beth stood up slowly, gazed up at the sky and said nothing, then turned, walked past her mother without even a glance, opened the kitchen door and disappeared into the house. Jill sat and rocked, gave her a while to get settled, then went back inside herself. Walking down the short hall from the kitchen, she noticed that Sam was no longer sleeping in front of her door. She walked back into the kitchen and looked in the utility room where Sam was lying half in his bed and half out, his head lying in the middle of a large pool of vomit and blood. She ran to his side and touched his cold, hardened body. Sam was dead.

Jill jolted up in bed in a sweating panic. It took a minute for the fog of her dream to clear, and even once she became aware that it wasn't real, that Sam was not dead, she suddenly felt in desperate need of a drink. She threw the covers off the bed and walked softly and quietly down the hall to look for one, towards the kitchen, hoping that no one else was up. She noticed that the sun was starting to come up, grey morning light seeping through the windows.

She saw Sam standing at the kitchen door, wanting to be let out, his tail drooped low, almost dragging the floor. She slowly opened the door. No squeak, Percy would have seen to that. She watched Sam bounce down the steps into the yard, then suddenly stop, arch his back upward and empty his stomach into a steaming pile on the ground. She shut the door behind her and went to him. He responded to her by wagging his tail a bit, but didn't seem anxious to play. They both walked back up the steps together. Sam jumped up on the sliding swing. Jill sat down beside him and he placed his heavy head in her lap. As she scratched the fur on his head she forgot about the drink. They watched the sunrise together instead.

◇ **29** ◇

"No such thing as luck"

Percy had a restless night and woke up at 5:30. He laid still and watched Beth sleeping, wondering what was going through her mind. She had said virtually nothing to him about her mother's sudden presence in their lives, acting as if it wasn't worth discussing; such an odd reaction from one so opinionated and never at a loss for words. By the time the sun began to shine through the shades, Percy gave up on sleep and went to the kitchen for coffee. There, he noticed that Sam wasn't in his bed, peeked through the screen door and saw the two of them together on the swing. He poured two cups of coffee and walked out to the deck.

"Good morning," he said as he handed her a cup. Sam wagged his tail vigorously at the sound of his voice, but didn't lift his head from her lap.

"Your dog threw up a minute ago."

Percy had been concerned after dinner the previous night when Sam showed no interest in playing catch. He had been lethargic ever since Caritas, maybe he had eaten too many scraps from the table. "He hasn't been feeling well for a couple of days now," Percy offered, "but he sure does love you."

Percy took a sip of coffee and watched Jill gently scratching Sam's head. He watched her closely and saw the fascination in her eyes that anything, even a dog, could possibly love someone like her. Then he heard himself say, "What are the odds?"

Jill looked at him for the first time and asked, "What odds?"

Percy smiled at her. "What are the odds that of all the people at church the other night, Sam would pick you, the woman who just happened to be Beth's mother?" He took another sip of coffee. "Jill, do you believe in luck?"

Jill continued scratching Sam for a while, then reached over and picked up her cup from the end table and took a sip, then fell again into silence. Minutes passed and Percy had about decided to let it go when Jill suddenly answered in a firm voice, "I believe in bad luck."

"I don't believe in any kind of luck," Percy added without explanation.

A couple more minutes passed, and just about the time Percy thought that the conversation was over, Jill began, "Actually, that was a bullshit answer I gave you earlier. There's no such thing as luck, good or bad. I think what I believe is that *in the end*, people get what they deserve in this life."

Percy thought for a moment, then answered, "I deserve a lot worse than what I've gotten in life. When I think about what I've done in the past and look at my life now, I can't say that I deserve many of the good things."

"I said that in the end people get what they deserve. What are you, 35? You ain't at the end yet."

"Maybe you aren't either."

"I'm a lot closer than you."

They both managed to smile. It was during this morning conversation on the deck that Percy decided that he would not take her to the doctor to validate her cancer claim. He would convince Beth somehow that it wasn't necessary, that they could find a way to contact Jill's doctor and have her records sent. Percy had no doubt that Jill was telling the truth, but it was a frail trust built upon intuition alone. He felt he could see the truth in her eyes. Even if Beth objected, they would find out sooner by getting her records than having to wait a week for an appointment and then another week for the results to come back.

As Beth slept in, Percy spent the morning discovering that Jill lived in Baltimore, where she stayed in a boarding house and subsisted on food stamps and other forms of public assistance and received her health care from a free clinic manned by interns and volunteer nurses from Johns Hopkins. It would be difficult to track them down, but after several phone calls, he had put Jill on the line to make the request. The woman from the records department promised to mail them out in a day or two.

When Beth awoke around noon, she offered no resistance to the new plan, a reaction that surprised Percy. Beth seemed to have become a silent, opinionless observer, content to let the appearance of her mother play itself out in front of her from a safe, uncommitted distance.

Percy was busy making BLTs for lunch while Jill and Beth sat at the kitchen table, when the uncomfortable silence was broken with, "Mom, since you're going to be here for a while longer, why don't you let me take you shopping for some clothes today?"

Jill looked up at Percy in astonishment, then at Beth in wonder at the words and the tone. Did her daughter just ask her to go shopping? Percy broke in quickly, "That's a great idea, Beth. I need to take Sam to the vet anyway, and you definitely need some clothes, Jill."

Jill's mind was racing, not only shopping, but shopping just the two of them. "That would be nice. Most of my things are in Baltimore, but honestly, I could have brought all of my clothes with me in one large plastic Target bag. I sure could use something new."

Percy stood at the front door and watched them drive away in the Mercedes; two smiles visible through the windshield, and found himself whispering a prayer of thanks to a God he hadn't spoken a kind word to in over ten years. Then he called to Sam, "Want to go for a ride in the truck?" Sam bounded past him with more energy than he had displayed in days, ran around the house and waited for Percy at the passenger door. Percy jumped up into the cab, fiddled with his iPod until Tom Petty and the Heartbreakers were blaring through the speakers. "Ok, boy, let's go find out what this throwing up is all about."

Beth had watched her mother pick out clothes and try them on in silence mostly, not quite sure what to say or how she should feel. She watched her try on pants and blouses, skirts, dresses and shoes. Everything had made her look 20 years younger. She saw the timid smiles, the wonder at what a miraculous turn her life had taken. They had eaten lunch together at Harry's, and when Billy had walked up and asked who her friend was, she had been surprised at how nice it had felt to say, "Billy, this is my mother."

They had enjoyed lunch, conversation had been easy, and they had managed to make each other laugh. Beth had come up with the idea to go get a haircut and a manicure. "I remember how beautiful your hair used to be. Let's see if we can bring it back."

Jill had made her laugh out loud with her response, "So, this hairdresser of yours can make me 25 again?"

Beth watched as the stylist went to work washing, cutting, and shaping. Jill had asked for her chair to be turned away from the mirror. She had felt too self conscious to watch, too embarrassed at what her life had done to her face and hair. She hadn't been prepared for how moving it had been to feel someone else's hands holding her head, washing her hair. She fought back tears as the stylist gently combed out her clean, wet hair, and could barely speak when she had called out to

Beth, "Your mother has the most beautiful head of hair I've seen in quite some time!" When it was done, her chair was turned around to face the mirror. Jill had looked and immediately covered her face with both hands to hide the tears. It couldn't possibly be real. She didn't recognize herself, couldn't believe that there was this much left of her. It was almost as if her last ten years of hell had been a dream. Beth had come to her side and hugged her long and hard, stopping only to say, "Now we need to get that manicure!"

By the time the call had come, the two of them were giggling like schoolgirls, telling jokes and making fun of the models in the haircut magazines.

Percy had gotten someone at the vet's office to look at Sam. They took blood samples, urine samples and a couple of x-rays. Nothing looked wrong on the outside, but they thought it wise to check him over thoroughly. Percy had explained his symptoms, and the young intern had listened carefully, explaining that Dr. Mitchell was on vacation, but that the blood work would be back in a day or so, and they would know more then.

"What are the possibilities? What *could* it be?" Percy had finally asked.

"Well, since we don't have much history on Sam, we don't even know how old he is, etc. It's very hard to say. Could be some sort of tick-borne illness, could just be food poisoning, or it might be cancer. But there isn't any point in dreaming up trouble. Let's just wait for the tests to come back, and then I'll give you a call."

As soon as the word "cancer" had come out of the intern's mouth, Percy's cell phone rang. It was Beth telling him that Dave had called. Melinda had gone into labor about a month and a half early, but there was no turning back. She and her "mom" were heading over to the hospital. Percy had immediately dropped Sam off at the house and gone to meet them. When he walked into the maternity waiting room, he saw them all over in the corner, Beth, Jill, and several people from church, hugging each other and laughing. He stopped in the doorway for a minute before they noticed him. Jill looked like something beautiful and new, and Beth stood beside her, looking very much like her daughter, smiling broadly and holding her hand. Percy wanted the moment to last forever. Beth glanced towards the door, saw Percy and quickly turned Jill around to face him as if to say, "Look! Look at my beautiful mother!!"

Percy mouthed the word, "WOW" across the room as the rude and stubborn thought passed through his mind, "I wonder how long she has..."

◇ 30 ◇

The Healing

Percy opened the heavy lid of the grill and smoke poured out in thick clouds. Two steaks, three hamburgers, and five hot dogs needed his attention, but Percy was lost in thought. Three summers had come and gone since the day that had changed everything. As he began fiddling with the meat, Percy thought about how odd it was that a man could live a life full of days without taking from them a single memory, but then suddenly a day comes along that explains everything that came before and informs everything that comes after. Most days are as predictable as the tides, and indistinguishable from any other, so infrequent are transformative moments. Then you wake up one morning, and by the time the sun sets your life has been changed in a thousand ways. The hope of such a thing is the reason we keep waking up.

Percy remembered going to the hospital. Melinda had gone into labor. Jill had gone shopping with Beth and looked amazing after a haircut and new clothes. He remembered thinking how beautiful they looked from across the room, standing next to each other. After a while, the doctors had managed to get Melinda in a holding pattern. It would be 48 hours before she finally gave birth to a son, Caleb Alexander, born six weeks premature and not much bigger than a shoe. He, Beth and Jill had been waiting at the hospital most of the day, getting updates from Dave. After meeting the baby, everyone was exhausted. They drove back home and pulled into the driveway just as the mailman was pulling away from the box. Percy sorted through it and found a fat envelope from Johns Hopkins and quickly hid it among the sales fliers from Lowe's and Home Depot. He walked into the house to find the message light blinking on the phone in the kitchen. It was from the vet's office, "Call concerning Sam's results." Where was Sam? Had they left him in the back yard all this time? Luckily, it was a beautiful day, not too hot. Percy had walked out on the deck and called for him. It was at that moment when the world went black, fell silent and slowed to a crawl. Sam was in the back corner of the yard, laying still and heavy on the very spot where he had entered Percy's life, in the shadow of the forsythia bushes. Percy had run down the steps and across the yard and fallen on the ground beside him. Sam was dead; his mouth opened slightly, his eyes dry like dusty marbles, his body cold and stiff.

Beth had found them together a few minutes later, Percy holding Sam in his lap, rocking back and forth, with tears trailing down his face. Soon Jill was there looking down at the three of them, sick with grief herself. She had never liked dogs, never even been around one her entire life until Sam had chosen her out of an old warehouse full of rejects. And now he was gone, like everything else she had ever loved.

Beth went back into the house and called the vet's office. Sam's blood work had shown cancer all through his body at quite an advanced stage. They had called to tell Percy that Sam didn't have much time left. After recovering from the initial blow, Percy had set about preparing the dog's body for burial. He gently wrapped him in his favorite blanket, the one that he had folded up and placed on the deck under the awning that very first night. Beth helped lift his body and then wrapped it tightly around him. Jill stayed a safe distance away, not wanting to be noticed.

Percy then asked if they would leave him alone. Beth and Jill disappeared into the kitchen while Percy got his dad's old grubbing hoe and shovel from the shed. He would dig a grave on the spot he had first seen him, and the place where he had passed. Once it was done, Percy raked the freshly turned soil with a leaf rake, clearing away the heavier clods of dirt until it was smooth and respectful. Someday soon he would buy some sort of marker to place on the grave.

Sam had flashed into his life and lit it up like a meteor shower for only a few short months. Whether it was chance or some divine appointment, Percy didn't know, but Sam had brought something precious with him. He had given Percy someone to care for, a reason to be better. He never spoke a word but seemed to understand everything. In just a few months Percy had given and received love in abundance, freely, holding back nothing. And now Sam lay cold and alone under three feet of red clay, gone forever.

Beth met him at the kitchen door, hugged him, and whispered, "We're going to miss him so much." Then, after a minute, "Mom does have cancer, cancer of the pancreas, just like she said. From what I can tell, it's pretty bad."

"I was almost hoping that she was lying about it, but I think I knew she wasn't. Have you said anything to her?" Percy looked past her and didn't see Jill anywhere.

"Yes, we looked at the records together. She went to her room to lie down. She's very upset about Sam. She really felt close to him."

The rest of the night had been uneventful, Sam's death having cast a pall over the house. Jill had eventually come out of her room, fixed herself a sandwich and settled down in the library on the love seat to watch some television, but nothing interested her, so she turned in early. Beth too, went to bed early, leaving Percy alone in his Herman Miller chair after making him promise that he wouldn't be too long.

Percy had rummaged through his books looking for something to read, but nothing appealed to him. Whenever that happened, he always ended up with Shakespeare. He skimmed the first few pages of The Merchant of Venice, but threw it aside. He picked up his dog-eared paperback, Hamlet, flipped over to his tortured first soliloquy and found the familiar phrases, *"'tis a consummation devoutly to be wish'd. To die, to sleep; to sleep: perchance to dream; ay, there's the rub."*

Still, thoughts of Sam would drift into the ancient text, the fresh pain of loss surprised Percy with its intensity. He hadn't remembered feeling this way even when his parents had passed. Sam seemed so innocent and undeserving of such a fate, to die alone and unattended by the person he had saved from a life of brooding self pity.

More Hamlet brought more memories of Sam. Suddenly it was after midnight, and Percy was hungry. He grabbed a beer and a bag of Doritos and stepped out on the deck. It had become humid and the sliding swing was damp to the touch, but he sat anyway. The air felt heavy, and the sky seemed especially low and black as coal.

Gilbert pulled out a chair from the table without a sound, sat down, crossed his legs and asked, "How can you eat those things?"

"I don't know why I like them so much," Percy answered. "I know they're terrible for me."

Gilbert smiled and shook his head. "Sorry to hear about Sam."

The only sound being made was the chomping of Percy's teeth grinding the orange chips, his fingers now dusted with the powdered spices of whatever the hell was in a Dorito. "How's Mom?"

"Good. Mom's good."

Hamlet sneered, *"A little more than kin, and less than kind!"*

Percy offered the bag to Gilbert. "Come on, try one! I bet you'll like it." Gilbert was gone. Percy walked back into the kitchen, threw the empty bag in the trash and washed the dust off his hands.

Back in the library, Gilbert sat in the Herman Miller, looked up at Percy and asked, "So, how much money did you pay for this?"

"You really don't want to know." Percy flopped down on the love seat, worn out from the day. "Why are you here, Pop? Why now?"

"I'm here to plant a thought in that thick skull of yours. Maybe this works, maybe it doesn't, but here goes. Your mother-in-law doesn't have cancer anymore. She's been healed. When you take her to the doctor to have her checked, he will tell you that she is cancer-free. The cancer she had was taken from her by your dog, Sam. He licked her hands clean of it and took it all away. And yes, it killed him, but he did it willingly. In fact, it was the very reason he was sent to you; it was his purpose, his destiny. Don't trouble yourself trying to understand it, and don't dishonor it with grief. All things work together for good, Son."

Hamlet sighed and then, *"What a piece of work is man, how noble in reason, how infinite in faculty, in form and moving, how express and admirable, in action, how like an angel."*

The next morning, Percy had slept late, and then woke with a start just before noon. His first thought had been of his dream. And now, three years later, he smiled at the memory as he flipped burgers and looked across his back yard. There was Dave with Caleb on his shoulders, trying to touch the low hanging leaves of the maple tree in the middle of the yard. Dave had been the one to suggest that Percy and Beth hold their wedding in the backyard of 16 Jennings Lane in the first place. It was a great idea. He had performed the ceremony under that very tree.

Beth had surprised Percy with her desire to sell her house

and make their life together in his old, cramped rancher in such an older neighborhood. She had explained that she wanted a break from the past, and especially her house and the greed and selfishness that it represented. Besides, she had said, it had never felt like home. Although her real estate license was still active, she refused to be involved or compensated for its sale. In a brilliant move, Melinda had suggested using JoJo as the listing agent. He had agreed to a reduced commission, and Percy had promised not to throw anything at him.

The windfall profit from the sale had guaranteed their future and left them with no plausible reason to delay starting a family. Jillian Frances Hope had been born a year later, and now she was giving her grandmother fits as a two-year-old. They had built an addition onto the back of the house to accommodate Jill, a mother-in-law wing with a private entrance, a deliberate symbol of their confidence in her sobriety, which, along with the cancer, had apparently been siphoned from her by Sam's soft pink tongue. Percy had told no one of the dream, just acted on its message, and let God have the credit.

Percy looked to Sam's corner of the yard and saw Beth and Melinda together, looking down at the flat stone marker that Percy had placed on his grave.

"We Love You, Dear Sam."

About Atmosphere Press

Founded in 2015, Atmosphere Press was built on the principles of Honesty, Transparency, Professionalism, Kindness, and Making Your Book Awesome. As an ethical and author-friendly hybrid press, we stay true to that founding mission today.

If you're a reader, enter our giveaway for a free book here:

SCAN TO ENTER
BOOK GIVEAWAY

If you're a writer, submit your manuscript for consideration here:

SCAN TO SUBMIT
MANUSCRIPT

And always feel free to visit Atmosphere Press and our authors online at atmospherepress.com. See you there soon!

About the Author

Doug Dunnevant has enjoyed writing and telling stories for most of his life and is pleased to debut his first published novel, *A Life of Dreams*. In 2014 he published his first book, *Finishing Well* — the story of caring for his aging parents during the final years of their lives. As author of the "The Tempest," he has blogged about sports, politics, his family, and the poignancy and hilarity of everyday life since 2011.

Doug lives in Richmond, Virginia but spends as much time as he can on a lake in Maine with his wife, Pam, and their adorable but neurotic golden retriever, Lucy.